Findi[illegible]
Pack

Greycoast Pack

Book One

Jena Wade
Lorelei M. Hart

Published in the United States of America

www.thejenawade.com

Prologue

Byrom

I had been attending the Beta meetings with my father and his Betas for years now. Ever since I could remember. I attended first as a young child, sitting at their feet, just listening and trying to understand the discussion, then as a young shifter, with the knowledge that I'd be Alpha of the pack someday. And now, I sat in on the meetings, not as an observer, but as the prospective Alpha.

My father announced his retirement plans a few moons prior. I would be taking the position within the next year. I wasn't ready. I didn't know if I would ever be ready. How would I ever fill my father's paws?

"I'm just saying that I don't think the pack can wait anymore." My father sat at the head of the table. His gaze bore into me, but I refused to cower under it.

"Wait anymore? I'm not that old, Dad. It's not fair to me to just pick a mate at random." I wanted to meet my fated mate. It was a dream of mine, one that I didn't want to give up just to be the Alpha. Perhaps that was selfish of me.

My dad had been lucky. He'd met his fated as a pup. He and my omega father grew up together.

I hadn't met mine, and so far, I didn't anyone in my generation who had met their fated yet.

"A leader needs to have an Alpha Omega, Byrom. It's our way. Choosing one of the omegas in the pack will be beneficial to you as an Alpha."

"You want me to take on a mate that I know is not chosen for me by fate, for the sake of the pack? What will happen when I do meet my fated?"

My father shook his head. "A leader makes sacrifices, Byrom."

"Byrom," Samuel, my father's most trusted Beta, spoke up. "If you don't have a mate when you take over as Alpha, it will leave you weak and vulnerable. Without an Alpha Omega at your side, things could get rough."

Samuel's son Rance had reminded me of that several times. The pinched look on Samuel's face told me he knew that Rance would be the one to cause the most trouble if I remained unmated.

I was the strongest alpha in the pack besides my father. Even my twin brother Lyle, born ten short minutes after me and identical to me in every other way, didn't match my strength.

I was the clear choice for the next alpha. But Rance didn't see it that way and had let me and everyone else know how he felt. It was only out of respect for his father that I didn't tear him apart.

"I don't know," I said. "I'll think it over."

My father stood, keeping his gaze trained on me. "Make a decision tonight," he said.

"That's so soon. I need more time."

"You've had your whole life to prepare, Byrom. Now it's time to start making the hard decisions. It's what this role requires. If you're the alpha I know you are, you'll make the right choice."

"That's unfair," I said, feeling more like a teenager than a wolf of twenty-eight years.

"Get used to it," he said. "You're going to be Alpha someday. Decisions are hard."

I growled and pushed away from the table.

"I expect a decision tomorrow morning," my father said. He glanced outside at the moon in the sky. "Come. We have a meeting with the Ashcliff Pack in forty minutes. If we leave now, we'll make it in time."

My omega father, the pack Alpha Omega, put a hand on my shoulder and squeezed. He'd remained silent during the meeting, like he always did. He spoke only when he needed to calm the group of Betas if they got too rowdy. "You will do the right thing, Byrom. I know you will."

I knew the power of having an Alpha Omega, had seen my dad steady the pack when they were distressed.

My father's Betas all left the room, walking out of the house before my father. He turned back to me.

"I know it's not any fun, Byrom. I know you want to meet your fated. I want that for you also. But sometimes an alpha puts the needs of the pack before himself. And that's what you need to do right now.

I nodded. "Yes, Alpha."

***

Hours later, I sat up on the roof of the pack house, looking out at the night sky.

I was curious about how the meeting with Ashcliff pack went. All I knew was that they were discussing ancient laws, but I had no idea which specific ones. I knew I'd be briefed in the morning. I didn't need to know right now.

Lyle climbed out the window and joined me on the roof. Over the years, the two of us had sat up here and talked many times. It was our spot.

"Thinking over which one of the pack members you're going to take as a mate?" he asked.

"Kiss my ass," I said. I sighed. "I can't think of any omega I'd want as a forever mate. What about you?"

He shook his head. "I don't even know if there's a fated out there for me. Doesn't seem like anybody's had a lot of luck lately with that sort of thing."

"Do you think there's a reason for that?" I asked. The topic has been weighing on my mind as I searched my memory for the last mating ceremony the pack had that featured a fated mate couple. It had been a while.

Lyle shrugged. "Could be. We keep ourselves pretty secluded. A vast majority of humans don't know we exists. We can't just all be fated to each other. Who's to say our fated mates aren't out there in the world, in another pack? Who's to say fated mates aren't just a figment of our imagination anyway?"

"Mine is out there," I said. My wolf howled. He knew our mate was out there, and he was anxious to find him.

Lyle snorted. "You're sure of that?"

"I am," I said. I trusted my wolf. He had never steered me wrong. "You don't think yours is?"

"Well, I'm not as sure as you are that one's just going to show up one day."

"I can feel it," I said. "I know he's out there."

"Well, I hope you find him, dude. Before it gets too late. Because Dad is right. You need a mate at your side in order to rule. It's the way."

My wolf growled low. "I know. I understand." I hated that I'd have to make the hard choice soon. If only I could convince my dad to give me more time. My fated was out there. I knew it; my wolf knew it. I didn't want to pick someone who wasn't him. But if I didn't find him soon, I wouldn't have a choice.

Headlights shined on the pack house as a car drove down the lane.

“Looks like they’re back,” Lyle said.

“It doesn’t look like the van,” I said.

The bubble lights of a police cruiser reflected in the moonlight. It was rare for them to stop out in our area, since we were sort of considered off limits to the local police. They gave us a wide berth, and we took it.

The police officer got out. Though I knew it was odd for us to be up on the roof, I couldn’t help myself.

“Can I help you?” I called out.

The officer jumped and looked up at Lyle and me standing on the roof. “I’m looking for anyone with the last name of Vicardi. I was told to contact someone named Byrom.”

“That’s me,” I said.

“I’m sorry to tell you, son. But there’s been an accident.”

Chapter One

Cord

Overdue!

The big red letters stamped on the outside of the electric bill jumped out at me as I sorted through the junk mail that accompanied it. I opened it to see how bad it was. Not that I had the money. But the dread of not knowing was too much.

“That’s not awful,” I lied to myself as the $313.21 past due plus fees balance stared at me. And that wasn’t even including this month’s bill, which was going to be added soon.

I checked my banking app to see how much I had. I’d been working hard at not spending money. Eating ramen—the cheap kind, not the good stuff—walking to work, not using lights when possible, pretty much everything I could think of. I did it all. Not that you could tell from my balance. When my check cleared, I’d have enough to keep my electricity going, but that was it.

I missed three days of work due to the stupid office being closed because of a fire alarm fail. I should not be penalized for their inability to maintain their building. And yet I was.

Oh, the joy of per diem work. Zero sick days, vacation days, or even *sorry we fucked you* days.

At least I had some applications in at the local bar. The tips would suck when happy hour included dollar beers, but it would be something. I'd held off for too long under a stupid sense of pride. *I went to college. I have a degree. I need to work in my field.* All bullshit. I had more student loans than I'd ever be able to pay off, and being snobby about the work I was doing wasn't going to accomplish jack shit.

And the loans were my fault. I listened to the counselor who told me repeatedly that being in foster care would make it so that the ratio of loans to grants would be doable and it was a necessary evil but worth it. They were not doable, not without the six-figure income I'd also been told would be easy to acquire. I'd been so gullible, or was it desperation? Desperate to make something of my life more than what my foster parents had repeatedly told me was my fate. After all, if my parents didn't want me, what good could I be?

Fuck that noise.

I backed out of my banking app and put the bill in my kitchen drawer, not wanting it to stare at me every time I walked by. I poured the last of the cereal into a bowl and stared at the less than a spoonful of crumbs. I dumped it into the garbage and looked through the fridge.

"A slice of generic American cheese and a pickle for

breakfast it is." And really, it didn't taste awful, not breakfasty, but not awful. I put a trip to the dollar store on my mental to-do list for the day. More ramen and a box or two of cereal should get me through the week.

The walk to work in the cool morning air did me well. I'd been craving the outdoors lately, which was so unlike me. I was never the person who wanted to go camping, and the bugs at picnics had me avoiding them more often than not, but lately? It was as if all of that had shifted, and suddenly, I needed the fresh air and green grass. I even considered going to the thrift store looking for a pair of hiking boots until work temporarily shut down, taking my income with it.

Run.

I shut down the stupid voice in my head. I needed to eat more. My lack of both calories and nutrition had been messing with me something fierce, and I kept hearing that single word, *run*, which was not something I ever longed to do. I was of the *if someone's not chasing you with an ax, you can walk, bro* mentality. Tell that to my low blood sugar hallucinating self. Maybe the dollar store would have some protein bars. That might help.

I was the first one at work, like always. My job started at eight o'clock, yet every day I clocked in at eight-oh-four because Adrianne, the person with the keys, the person without a timecard to punch, showed up exactly at eight. She had benefits, too. Not that I was jealous. Fine, I was beyond jealous. What I'd do for health insurance and sick days.

I leaned against the brick wall, waiting for Adrianne and

scrolling through my phone looking for job leads. Nothing new. Maybe the bar would call today.

"You're here early." Adrianne startled me from my job search. It was seven fifty-nine. Hardly early. "Anything good?" She pointed to my phone, and since she was my supervisor of sorts, I lied.

"Naw. I was just looking for some hiking boots in the local for-sale groups." I pushed back from the wall as she fumbled with her keys.

"You like hiking?"

"I guess."

"My ex left his boots at my place. They're a twelve. If you want them, they're yours." She opened the door. "It will be good to get the rest of his shit out of my place."

"How much?" I was an eleven and a half, but they could work. I'd probably end up hating it anyway.

"They were really expensive. So expensive that Don told me that he couldn't buy me a birthday present so he could afford them, so if you give me a penny that I can mail him, that should be perfect." *Don't mess with Adrianne. Got it.*

"I can do that. I'm going to clock in and get to work." I gave her my best smile. "You're made of amazing."

"If you think I'm amazing after seeing my bitchy side, I like you. Maybe you can be my wingman one night at Ralf's?"

“I applied there,” I confessed. “For nighttime, obviously.”

“Because they pay you per diem people shit here,” she corrected me. “I’ll tell Ralf you’re a keeper. He owes me after setting me up with Don.” She winked. “Besides, you can be a good wingman from the bar.”

I clocked in and headed to my tiny cubicle. The day was looking up. I had a possible in for the job I wanted, I was getting new boots, and I’d made my first maybe friend at the office. Maybe things would be okay, and I wouldn’t end up in an even dumpier apartment, or worse.

I just needed a couple of shifts a week and a little bit of luck and things would be okay. That wasn’t too much to ask for, was it?

Chapter Two

Byrom

I gathered the paperwork that I'd need for the meeting I'd scheduled with my Betas. I checked my watch; they should be arriving anytime.

Lyle, my twin and most trusted Beta, already paced outside the packhouse, just waiting for me to join him. Our meetings were informal; we didn't have a boardroom or even a designated meeting space. We just gathered outside most of the time, sometimes in the forest, sometimes outside the packhouse, for a quick meeting of the minds.

My father, late Alpha of the Greycoast Pack, had never needed notes or a to-do list or an agenda for his meetings with his Betas. His meetings were quick, to the point, and his Betas hung on his every word like it was gospel. He had been a strong leader, and the pack had followed his lead and trusted him completely. He steered them well and made our pack one of the strongest in the state, maybe even the nation. He was a true leader, a thousand times better than I was.

But he was gone now. And it was up to me to lead the

pack through this difficult time. My father had trusted me with that responsibility. As the eldest alpha son, it was my job to take on the role as Alpha. I'd known the day was coming but had no idea it would be here so soon. I'd been pushing back against the position and then suddenly it was thrust upon me.

The night my fathers met their abrupt and unfortunate end threw my world into a tailspin. I didn't even have the luxury of having my father's Betas to assist me, since they too had passed in the tragic accident that had taken both my parents from me. One tractor trailer losing control took an entire generation of leadership from our pack. There wasn't much left of the van that had held my fathers and their Betas.

I stepped out onto the deck of the main packhouse. The Alpha's house. My house. This was where I lived and had lived for my entire life. A place that had once been full of love and laughter was now empty and quiet.

Sure, pack members still visited. We had an open-door policy; anyone was welcome to come in and use the main house as their own, but then they'd leave and go to their own homes. And I was left in stark emptiness. Five bedrooms, four bathrooms, a lavish kitchen equipped to make food for an army, but it was just me there at night. Alone.

Lyle nodded to me and stood at attention when I came outside. Though he was my brother, only younger than me by ten minutes, he never wanted the Alpha position and instead made it clear that he was happy with his status as my Beta.

My other Betas arrived one by one. Gio, a quiet, strong wolf that I trusted almost as much as my twin. We were the same age, and while we grew up together, we weren't exactly friends. Gio kept to himself, but I knew I had his support. Kade, our resident goofball. He made jokes and had a good time. He helped to keep the mood light. But when push came to shove, I knew he could turn serious and be a strong Beta. And last, just a few seconds late, enough to annoy me but not enough that I could say something, Rance.

Since taking over, Rance had become even more vocal about his lack of trust in my leadership. Out of respect for Samuel, and the idea that I'd need Betas who weren't afraid to challenge me, I'd asked Rance to be mine. His father had been my father's Beta, and he'd been a good one, but somehow Rance was a bad apple that had fallen far on the wrong side of the tree. He'd caused trouble even before the pack had lost their highest leaders, and now, instead of helping to bring the pack together, he sought to tear us apart.

"All right, guys," I said, and I looked at my paperwork. "Let's talk about our schedule for the coming week. Gio, you're continuing to help build the new house for Laurence and his pups, right?"

Gio nodded.

"Everything's going fine with that?"

He nodded again. "I have to make a trip to town to pick up supplies. I'll take Laurence with me; it shouldn't take long."

"Great," I said. "Keep me updated. I'll swing by this afternoon and lend a hand. Lyle, you'll cover perimeter duty when Gio has to go to town."

Lyle nodded.

I had each Beta bring me up to speed on a few more things related to the pack life. Our pack was strong and healthy and had been for years thanks to my father's leadership. We were secluded in our woods, but we still utilized the local town for supplies. Most of the townspeople thought we were some kind of weird hippie cult. If only they knew the truth.

Kade filled us in on the school schedule. Our classroom work was half inside, half outdoors. Our wolf nature craved the outdoors, and it wasn't easy to keep young pups contained. Though they couldn't shift until puberty, their wolves were still present inside them, and they would drive a human teacher bonkers.

I had to cut Kade off before he got too far off-topic. "All right, I think that's everything for today."

"Are you sure?" Rance said with a sneer. He hadn't had any information to report to me, which meant either he wasn't doing his job as a Beta and keeping up to date on the pack happenings or he was just being a dick. Either was likely. "There's nothing else on your little list there?"

I growled and then took a deep breath. He acted like I had snapped at him, backing away and holding up his hands in surrender.

"Hey, easy, man."

Lyle clapped me on the back and flanked my right side. An innocent gesture, but it assured me he had my back if Rance got out of line. "Not getting enough sleep?"

I knew my twin well enough to know he was changing the topic in an attempt to de-escalate the situation. "I'm fine. Do you have something to share, Rance?"

"The full moon is coming up. It'll be a full month that you've been Alpha."

"Yes, I know. What of it?" It had been twenty-seven days since my parents had passed. I didn't need a reminder about how long I'd been without them.

He shrugged. "About time you took a mate, don't you think? The pack needs an Alpha Omega."

I growled again, this time watching through my wolf's eyes. If he was going to be so belligerent, let him see just how close he was to being challenged, a challenge his wolf would lose before it began. "I can lead without a mate."

This time Rance didn't back down. He squared off. Did the man have a death wish? "Are you sure about that?" His fingers clenched into a fist.

"Back down, Rance," I commanded, infusing my Alpha strength into my voice to let him see I meant business. "There is no law that states the Alpha must be mated."

"There never has been an unmated Alpha. The law doesn't need to be written. That's just the way it is." And he well knew that. I'd regret making him a Beta if I thought for half a second it would be better with him on the outside of my leadership ring. He'd be the one to cause an insurgence from the bottom, using gossip to gather support. Not that this was the safest place for him to be.

Blood.

Or there was my wolf's plan, which on days like this I was on board with.

Kade stepped between the two of us. "Both of you need to go out and get laid." He laughed and pushed at Rance's chest like we were all just goofing around.

We weren't, and everyone in the room was well aware. I needed to do something about Rance, but not today. Kade was right on that.

My wolf clamored inside me. It had been restless for a while now. Due to the stress of taking over the new pack or losing my parents? It was hard to tell. Either way, I needed to go for a run.

"This meeting is adjourned," I said. "Rance, why don't you make sure the firewood is all stacked? The nights are getting colder, and I don't want anyone in the pack without heat." Let him have some physical work to tame his wolf a bit.

He narrowed his eyes at me. "I don't think I'm on the schedule for that."

"Do it anyway," I said. With him, I knew I had to show him who was the boss or he would walk all over me. And if that meant giving him shit work when he got out of line like this, that's what was going to happen.

I began stripping off my clothes. “I’m going for a run; I expect the job to be done when I get back.”

I shifted, fur covering me as my body changed its form. I was happiest as a wolf these days. In a way, I felt closer to my parents when I was in wolf form, like our spirits were still connected.

The restlessness never fully went away, though, no matter how long I ran or how tired my limbs were. My wolf sought out something. I just wasn’t sure what that something was.

Chapter Three

Cord

It had been just over a week since Adrianne and I had forged our sort-of friendship, and things had started to brighten in my life. I had been able to pick up one shift a week at the bar on a trial basis, and the first night I made enough to buy real food for the week, leaving my other paycheck for my bills.

I didn't hate the job, not that one night was enough to tell, really, but the people were nice, and the money was good, and there was something about being surrounded by people who were having fun and being social. I spent my days in a tiny cubicle with zero personal items since I technically didn't work there and my nights going home to an empty, shitty apartment. This was good. I could feel it.

Adrianne also came through with the boots, which fit perfectly. She went so far as to write out a receipt for them for the grand total of one penny. She was a good one to have on my side and one I definitely wanted to stay that way. If only I had thought to be chattier with her earlier. It was nice to have a friend.

I laced up my boots and headed out into the day. It was overcast and cool, perfect hiking weather. Although I wasn't sure if what I had been doing was technically hiking. Mostly I just wandered in the woods, sat under trees, and smelled a lot of things. And yeah, the last part was weird but also calming, so I went with it.

The hiking had started as a walk when I first got up and had quickly morphed to a twice-a-day activity, and it gave me a sense of peace I hadn't had…ever in my memories.

Maybe I should've been a forestry major instead of earning the ever generic and utterly useless business degree. Apparently, you needed a masters for it to be worth anything, and taking out more debt to possibly get a better job was not in my future. I learned that lesson already.

I slid a protein bar into my pocket and grabbed a bottle of water. I didn't have to work today and planned to stay out until I was bored or it rained. Maybe I'd stay out even if it rained. It was warm enough that I wouldn't get too chilled.

I started into the woods at the same place I always did, but instead of turning left and heading toward the stream, I found myself going right in the direction of a large hill. Or was it a small mountain? I'd never been good at geography, and I had a belt scar on the back of my thigh to prove it; my foster parents hadn't been the perfect family they pretended to be.

Run.

It was back. The voice, the one that I'd blamed on blood sugar, then blamed on exhaustion, and now…there was nothing left to blame it on other than losing my mind. I needed to see someone about it. I knew this. But counseling cost money even with insurance, which I didn't have.

And really, I'd done the counseling thing as a kid when my foster parents said I heard voices and talked back to them. I'd been given pills, pills that had me falling asleep in class. The entire time period was almost a blur. I didn't even remember hearing anything. But now? Now I was beginning to wonder if maybe it was the same voice coming back.

Run.

I ignored it. What was the point in answering myself? There wasn't any. It had only led to problems in my past. Too bad it didn't stay there.

The forest got denser and denser, the scents stronger and stronger as I kept moving forward, continuing to ignore the voice. I had no desire to run. I enjoyed a leisurely pace as I took in the new flowers blooming, the birds singing, and the way the moss formed almost little magical villages on the fallen trees.

This was where I belonged. Maybe after I got my shit together, I could save enough for a bit of land and a cabin.

Run.

Mate.

Run.

Mate? That was new.

"What do you mean, mate?" And just like that, I broke my vow to ignore the voice.

Mate. Run. Mate. Mate. Mate.

And the answer meant absolutely nothing until it meant everything. I fell to the ground, needing my boots off, my feet suddenly suffocating. It didn't help, the feeling only growing until the pain grew so strong, I bellowed out in agony as the sound of my clothing ripping echoed in my ears.

Run. Mate. Run. Louder and louder until I found myself on my hands and knees, only they weren't my hands and knees anymore. They were—I couldn't even think the word. The fur and nails in my vision were too much to handle. Then suddenly, I was no longer there, or rather I was there, but far away.

Run. Run. Run. The voice was now in front of me. I tried to move, but nothing happened. I was no longer in control of anything. Was I dead? Was this death?

My body—or at least what my body had become—took off like a shot, his feet hitting the ground with a thud with every step as he sped through the woods. I was a spectator, but from the inside, unable to take any control over what was happening.

Please let this not be death.

Running, running, running, never slowing. The voice was

on a mission to get somewhere. I just didn't know where and was terrified to find out.

I'd been right to be scared as I came to a halt. Or was it he? Or we? It didn't matter. The only thing that did was the group of wolves that stood between the trees, and none of them looked happy to see me—us—their teeth bared and their ears back.

My head snapped to the side, and there stood a wolf, much larger than the others save one, his blend of grey and white fur blowing in the wind. With my sharpened vision, it was as if I could see every strand.

Safe.

"Yes," I agreed. He was safe. The biggest, scariest wolf of all was safe. I didn't know how I knew or why it even mattered since I was about to be torn to shreds.

The wolves with the bared teeth stepped forward. No, scratch that, most of them circled me, and my safe wolf backed off, as another wolf's body, a wolf almost his size, pushed him away like a bodyguard might move their charge away from danger. But I wasn't dangerous. I wanted to fight to get to him, needing to be with him even if only for a second, before my life was ended in the vile way I imagined was coming. I pushed, trying to regain control of my body, this body.

I failed and found myself cowering on the ground with my head tilted to the side, exposing my neck.

I was fucked.

Chapter Four

Byrom

I resisted as Lyle flanked my right side and pushed me away from the unknown wolf. What had begun as a normal pack run quickly turned into something else when we'd spotted another wolf trespassing on our land.

I didn't get a good glimpse of him, but his scent called to me in a way that no other scent had. It was comforting, and it soothed my aching heart, but just as quickly as it had washed over me, it was gone.

The unknown wolf felt like family, like something familiar. But that didn't make any sense. I'd never seen him before. I didn't recognize the reddish tint to his fur. If I'd seen it before, I'd surely remember. I trusted him, but I had no idea who he was, had never seen him before.

Lyle continued to push at me until we were out of sight. It was a smart move, one we'd all been taught in our training: Protect the Alpha from the immediate threat while the Betas and other pack members take care of the rogue wolf, the danger.

Danger. He wasn't a danger. I'd bet my life on it. Lyle would not do the same, and had I tried to stop his extraction of me from the situation, he'd do exactly as he should and prevent it at all costs.

Once we were far enough away, I gave into my yearning and growled at Lyle, and he stopped pushing at me. I gestured toward the northern perimeter, and we took off. We at least needed to make sure that there were no other trespassers out here before heading back to the pack buildings. The rogue would be safe until I returned.

Not that I should want him safe. *Ours.* My wolf disagreed.

Two other pack members followed closely behind us. We were several hundred yards away from where we found the new wolf when I picked up an older scent. I recognized it as that of one of the Northbay Pack wolves. They were our neighbors and had always been amicable and respectful of the pack boundaries. Perhaps their friendliness had changed since we'd last spoken. It wasn't friendly to enter another pack's territory without permission, and this scent was well within our perimeter. It was several days old, which meant the wolf was long gone. But how had my scouts missed it?

Lyle picked up on the same thing, and he growled in anger. I barked at him to snap him back to focus as I made a mental note to ask at the next meeting with my Betas. There were more important things to worry about at the moment.

We moved along the rest of the perimeter, but nothing caught our noses.

Was the rogue wolf related to the Northbay Pack? Had

they sent him? I didn't smell the Northbay Pack on him, but there were ways to mask scent. Or worse? Had they used him, an outsider? I quickly dismissed the idea. The wolf wasn't dangerous. I felt it in my gut, and my wolf was in full agreement.

He was ours. The realization had my thumping loudly and my stomach doing somersaults. This shifter was ours. Why did he have to show up the way he did?

We weren't far from the packhouse when I slowed to a walk. I gestured for the other two pack members to keep going back to their homes, or they could do whatever they wanted. The pack run was officially over. I shifted back quickly to my human form, and Lyle followed suit.

"Everything all right?" he asked.

"I don't know. Did you catch that scent?" No way was I bringing up my newfound realization. Not going to happen.

"Yeah. Northbay." He looked to the north, towards their territory, eyes narrowed. "They've always been friendly with us when Dad was Alpha. Do you think that has changed?"

"I don't know. I'll have to set up a meeting with the Alpha there. We'll see what their deal is. They may know something about this wolf we just found." Even as I said it, I didn't like the idea. I had no intention of bringing this new wolf to the attention of another pack. He was mine. My wolf paced within me, anxious to get back to his side. I hadn't even gotten a good look at him, but I couldn't get him out of my mind. All I'd caught was the hint of red fur and a great deal of fear. I wanted to erase that fear from him. He needn't be afraid of my pack.

Except right now, he kind of did, and that had my wolf ready for blood.

"What's going on with him?" Lyle asked.

"What do you mean? I don't know anything about him." But I wanted to know everything.

"You were weird." Lyle had changed from speaking as my Beta to speaking as my brother, my twin. The change was so subtle, if anyone overheard us talking, they'd have no idea, yet it was there and gave me the comfort I needed right then.

I raised an eyebrow. "Excuse me?" I let a sliver of my Alpha power into my voice, too scared—no, scared wasn't the right word. Too apprehensive to let him in just yet.

"Don't give me that shit," he said, calling me on my shit just as a good brother should. I hated it. "I'm talking to you as a brother, not as your Beta right now. What's going on?"

I stepped back. He was right. Lyle was my twin, and I needed to remember that. The power as Alpha could go to a wolf's head, which was why having an Alpha Omega was important. They provided balance. I couldn't let my position as Alpha get to me. I needed to keep a level head, like my father always had. "There's something about him. His scent is familiar."

"I didn't notice it." He gave me side eye. Fair enough.

"Have you seen him before?"

"No, never. But it's like I know him." I could be honest with Lyle in a way that I wasn't with my other Betas. Not because I didn't trust them, but because I trusted Lyle that much more. And even at that, I couldn't share it all. Something was holding me back.

"You're going to have to follow protocol on this. If you don't, Rance will be all over your ass." Fucking Rance.

My chest rumbled with a low growl. The protocol would be to dispose of the lone wolf for trespassing if we couldn't find the pack that he belonged to. If we did find the pack that he belonged to, it would be up to their Alpha to punish him, unless foul play was suspected, and then it was war. Either which way, there were consequences for trespassing on another pack's land.

The thing was he didn't smell like any pack that I had ever encountered.

"No," I said. It wasn't a question or up for negotiation. He. Would. Not. Die.

"No?" Lyle asked, though it seemed as if he expected that reaction.

Mine. My wolf growled within, but I kept it contained.

I clenched my fists. "I can't," I said.

"You have to," Lyle insisted. As my Beta, it was his job to council me, advise me on what was best for the pack. Alphas who let power get to their heads were likely to go feral and not make good decisions that benefited the pack. Instead, they looked out only for themselves, for their wolves. I wouldn't be that type of Alpha, but I also wouldn't let antiquated practices dictate that I murder another wolf for no reason. Especially not this wolf. He was mine. He was special to me.

"I won't." I silently dared him to contradict me. He was wise enough to stay silent. "We'll find another way. I'm not killing a person who isn't a threat to us."

"We don't know that he isn't a threat." Did Lyle want me to lose my control? Because I was too close as it was.

"Then we will find out." I bit out the words through clenched teeth, hoping to keep my anger in check and my wolf at bay.

Lyle took a step back and bared his neck. "Okay. I understand. I'll support you. Many of the other pack members will as well. But just so you know, Rance is going to have a problem." He always did.

I nodded. "I'll deal with that when it comes up." I didn't dare say it out loud, but I'd sooner kill Rance than the beautiful wolf that we'd found on our land.

Chapter Five

Cord

Corralled.

I was corralled by the wolves and being taken. Though I didn't know where, I knew it wasn't good. It didn't take a brain surgeon to see that at least one of these wolves wanted me dead. He'd snapped at me, lunged at me even, only to be stopped by another. I had nicknamed him Evil Asshat wolf. But really, he might've been less asshat and more scared of me. Animals were like that. At least according to YouTube.

Shit. What if he wasn't an animal? What if none of them were? What if they were like me, just minding their own business and hiking and boom, they were wolves? Fuck. I was a wolf.

Had the whole world turned into wolves like some sort of wolf-pocalypse? Or was it more like zombies, where it only infected part of the population and the humans who remained had one job left, to rid the world of our kind? Aliens? So many possibilities and not one of them was good.

I followed them, not by choice, but because I still had no

control over my body. My four paws traipsed along, going to who knew where and to face who knew what fate.

At first, the nice wolf was there. But then…then he was gone, and so was the wolf who looked almost identical to him. Things would be better if Nice Wolf was there. I knew it—felt it in my bones. My bones that were no longer my own.

We walked for what felt like hours but was more realistically not even close to that, the dread of what was to come slowing each second into an eternity.

Finally, we reached a barn, and I was escorted inside. One by one, the wolves transformed into men, like it was the most normal thing in the world. Their bodies changed seamlessly from walking on four paws to standing on two legs. Not a one of them took their eyes off of me.

"Shift back," a man snarled from my left. He was standing there buck-ass naked wearing nothing but his grimacing look, one that told me he'd rather see me dead than obeying whatever it was he just commanded. "Shift. Back. Now. You vermin." The man kicked at me, his foot landing right on my ribcage, and I fell to the ground with a thud. I cried out from the pain, but it came out as a whimper.

I lay there, not sure what to do, even if I could do something. The voice or whatever it was that was controlling me didn't do anything, either.

"He told you to shift," a voice from the other side of me demanded.

"What is this?" A man walked into the barn, a pair of jeans slung low on his hips, his hair mussed with a leaf in it. A sense of calm washed over me at his voice. Was he—could he—this was Safe Wolf?

Mate.

That voice needed to shut up. We were in a crisis, and he was what? Begging for sex.

"I told the vermin to—" He was cut off by a snarl, a snarl coming from the man with the jeans, who was now flanked by another half-dressed man. The two were identical in looks, but something about the one with the commanding voice called to me.

Jealousy welled up in me at the second man, standing so close to what was mine. Whoa! Where did that come from? And yet, it felt true. So true. He was mine.

"Try again, Rance, and tread lightly. Don't think I have forgotten your transgression from earlier." Had he been speaking to me in that calm yet threatening tone, I'd have been pissing myself. The man was lethal; of that I had no doubt. And yet that feeling of safety still enveloped me in his presence. I no longer was positive that my last breath would be in this barn.

"I told the intruder to shift. He is defying me." He tilted his head ever so slightly.

"I concur, Alpha," the other man who had barked orders at me added. "The intruder is not cooperating."

"The intruder reeks of fear, and the two of you are only scaring him more. I never ordered you to force him to shift or threaten him in any way." He took a step closer, the man at his side doing the same.

"Sorry, Alpha. You're right." The nicer, but still terrifying guy took a step back, tilted his head to the side, and bared his neck.

Alpha. The safe man's name was Alpha. I thought back to the books I'd read about alpha males and how much of an asshole they all were, and yet here he stood, making me feel safe even as the others were doing anything but.

"Little wolf, I need you to take your skin, please," he said so calmly, so sweetly, I wanted to comply. "Shift." His voice was firmer but still not laced with the rage the man he called Rance's tone held.

My body started to shake, the pain from earlier flooding back into me, only this time more intense. Cracks and pops echoed in my head as I fell to the ground howling, howling that slowly turned into screaming, my ability to contain my pain nonexistent. It hurt so much that when it finally stopped, and I was in control once again, all I could do was curl up in a ball and sob. My muscles quivered at the residual pain, my body cold, then hot, then cold again, sweat pouring from me. It was too much.

"Little wolf." A calm flowed through me. "Little wolf, you need to stop."

"He needs to get up and face his consequences like a wolf." Rance turned his attention to me, his voice somehow eviler. "This cowering bullshit won't save you." The sound of his spitting hit me only a millisecond ahead of said spit.

“Stand. The. Fuck. Back.” This wasn’t Alpha. It was the man at his side. I didn’t know his name yet, but he was on my side as much as Alpha appeared to be. “You hit the Alpha with your spit, you disrespectful shit.” Or on Alpha’s side. I didn’t care which at that point. I just wanted the asshat wolf gone.

“Sit,” Alpha commanded, and I found myself complying without even thinking it through, like I had to please him. It hurt. Oh, how it hurt, but I bit my tongue, not wanting to show my weakness again.

“Tell me, little wolf, what pack are you from?” Alpha asked, his posture menacing, his tone not. Was the posture for me or the naked men? Shit. I was one of the naked men. I covered my cock and balls with my hands.

Two of the men, the nicer ones, chuckled at that as their junks just hung out there for all to see.

“I don’t know what you’re asking.” I sounded like me, but not, my throat a hot mess from the screaming and crying.

“Who is your Alpha?”

“I want to answer you, but I really don’t understand you.” He was Alpha. I didn’t know any other Alphas. What the fuck was going on?

“It doesn’t matter. You will die at moonrise.” Rance stomped away, calling over his shoulder. “Get over whatever softness you have for that wolf, Alpha. You know the laws. Break them and your reign is over. Better yet, let the shit live. We need a real Alpha around here.”

A growl built up in Alpha's chest, and whatever it meant to the others, they all tilted their heads and left, leaving me alone with the two with jeans on. Two naked men stood on either side of the doorway, their shadows darkening the opening.

"Let's get you where you need to be. We'll figure things out from there." He held his hand out for me, and I took it, my legs wobbly as I stood.

"Rance is right," the other man said as if I weren't there. "It is the law."

"It's not written law. Rance can kiss my ass. Anyone here can see this was his first shift. Look at the way his legs are wobbling like a day-old colt."

Whatever law they were talking about, it meant that I was going to die.

"Shift."

This time, I morphed into a wolf with more ease, the pain less, my mind at the forefront, no longer pushed back. Did the Alpha have some sort of power to make me transform? He must. But how?

"Take him to holding while I figure this all out."

Holding. That didn't sound good. That very much sounded the opposite of good.

And as I watched, Alpha and the one beside him shucked their clothing and mumbled something about taking one last border run. The man called Gio and a wolf stood on either side of me, Gio telling me to walk—walk to my death.

Chapter Six

Byrom

The main packhouse and homes of pack members sat nearly dead center of our territory, where we were safest. When Lyle and I made our way back from checking the other end of the perimeter, the place was abuzz with activity. We shifted back to our human forms. Many people were out of their homes, talking amongst themselves. They all quieted as I walked down the center of the dirt road that worked its way through the main part of our land.

"What are you gonna do with the trespasser?" Trevor asked. He was a young wolf just coming into his prime, only eighteen years old. Old enough to be curious, but still too young to hold his tongue. His father put a hand on his shoulder and whispered to him. I smiled to let them know I wasn't upset by the question.

A pack too afraid to ask their Alpha questions was a pack that lacked trust. My father's voice filled my head. I wished his voice came to me with solutions for fixing the problem with Rance and his insubordination.

Many of my Betas stood outside the barn we used for

storage but that also served as our holding area when necessary and where I'd told them to hold the rogue wolf for now.

Earlier, I'd wanted to take him back to my home and put him in my bed where he could rest and be safe. I wanted to feed him, comfort him, ease his fear, but that was not an option. Protocol needed to be followed, even if I hated it.

Now that I had time to think and clear my head, I still wanted to take him home with me. That didn't change, but at least now I could avoid looking rash in whatever decision I came to. Because the reality was I was no closer to a solution now than I was just a few hours earlier.

I nodded to Gio and Rance as Lyle and I walked in. Rance stood at attention, a nasty sneer on his face. Gods, I hated him.

"You come to take care of this trespasser, Alpha?" The way he said it held no respect. "How shall you do it? A club to the head? Tear his throat out with your teeth?" As if we clubbed people to death. He said it to scare the wolf, and anyone hearing him would draw the same conclusion. I'd blame his awfulness on his father's death, but Rance had always been wretched, even when he attempted to veil it for the sake of his father. Not that his father was much better.

"Stand down, Rance. We don't know anything about this man. I'm not going to kill him." Of that I was certain. I didn't have it in me. Not him. Rance, on the other hand, my wolf would take great pleasure in bleeding out.

I found our rogue shifted back into his human form. He was huddled in the corner of the holding cell. My stomach rolled as my gaze landed on him.

“We forced him to shift, and then he tried to fight his way through,” Gio said. “Rance hit him a few times. That’s it, Alpha.”

With swift movement, my hand flew on its own. The back of my hand struck Rance’s cheek, and he stumbled back. “That wasn’t necessary,” I growled. “Your disrespect is becoming unbearable, Rance. Change your attitude or find yourself gone from this pack.” I needed to facility option B quickly. I had no more patience left for him. None. There was zero chance that terrified wolf fought them. His fear was so palpable, it would’ve paralyzed him where he stood.

“We did what we had to do to protect our land. You need to do the same.” Rance glared at me, his eyes blazing with anger. He held his body as if he expected me to fight him. Eventually, he walked away. Gio followed once I gave him a nod. He’d make sure Rance didn’t return too quickly even without the exact command.

I caught Lyle’s gaze once we were alone with the unknown wolf.

“Something has to be done about Rance. If you won’t, either I or Gio will. We can’t stand back and watch our Alpha be treated with disrespect. Our wolves won’t allow it,” he said.

“His time is coming. I’ll either have him collared for punishment or banished soon enough.” Collaring was the worst punishment we could give; death was far more preferable. When we collared a wolf in the ways of our ancestors, they could no longer shift until set free. For us, it was a hell on earth and reserved for only the worst of crimes. It hadn't been used in my lifetime, and my father had called it too barbaric to be considered, but with Rance, I considered it all right.

But not now. Now I faced an even bigger challenge than Rance, and somehow, it felt more important. This trespasser, this familiar but unknown wolf that I had never seen before, that I didn't recognize in his human or his wolf form, that my wolf recognized as mine, I needed to figure out what to do with him.

The man no longer covered his head with his hands. He looked right at me, curiosity replacing the fear in his eyes. The blue orbs sparkled in the light of the barn.

"Can you stand?" I asked.

He nodded but didn't move.

"Will you please stand, little wolf?"

He did so. He stood straight, his legs slightly wobbly, and his hand over his junk. It was the second time he'd covered himself. What kind of shifter cared about nakedness? All of us in this room were naked; none of us had bothered to put on clothes after coming back from our run. The only reason I'd worn my jeans earlier was to piss off Rance. As much as I tried to convince both myself and Lyle that I didn't give a shit about his crap, I did, and that little bit of human I showed by grabbing my jeans would eat at him. My father would've told me not to poke the snake. My father wasn't here. If he was, said snake would still be robed in obedience. He was so much better at this Alpha thing than I ever would be.

I exchanged another glance with Lyle. He was just as confused as I was about the shifter's modesty. Even with this being a first shift, he had to have seen others shifting around him. Except maybe he hadn't. Some of his previous comments fell loosely into place, not enough to make complete sense of them, but enough to let me know where to begin once we got the omega home. Not that I should be taking him home, but fuck it. I was.

I stepped closer to the individual. He smelled vaguely of wolf, but mostly human. His scent was alluring, like walking into the forest after a fresh rain. Earthy, pure, and full of new life. An omega, not an alpha like me and Lyle.

My wolf howled within me.

Claim. Take. Mine. Mate.

Oh, fuck. Somehow, I knew deep down in my soul that our rogue, who was somehow more human than wolf, affiliated with no pack I recognized, was my mate. My omega mate.

This just all got a fuck-ton more complicated.

Chapter Seven

Cord

I woke, my body sore, my brain fuzzy, my mouth parched, wishing it had been a dream.

It was not.

I cracked my eyes a tad, trying to see if I was alone, finally blissfully alone. As they shoved me in here with a kick to the ass—or was it rump, since I was still in wolf form?—I'd been sick to my stomach thinking this was it, the end. Instead, they had just closed the door and walked away after the Rance guy kicked me a few more times.

The room really wasn't that bad for a barn. There was a small window, allowing some light in. Not small enough for even my small frame to crawl through, but still. It was something. The entire time, my wolf—for I finally understood the voice that haunted me on and off for all those years for what it was—kept chanting, "Mate."

I found myself pacing, not sure how to get back on my two feet, not sure about anything other than I was in deep shit. To think I'd been worried about bills. Bills were nothing compared to the shitstorm I was in now. They didn't seem that freaking important anymore. That was for sure.

And then the door cracked, and I knew…I just knew it was bad. There was something in the air that just smelled wrong. I backed into the corner, fully in control of my body but feeling something pushing at me to gain control. I couldn't let that happen again. If I was going to die, I wanted it to be with me fighting, not this wolf who invaded my being.

Your wolf.

He nipped at me from inside as the door opened just enough for Rance and some other guy to come in and close it behind them. Rance, who I recognized as the Asshat Wolf, looked mad. No, worse than mad, insane and rageful like in a horror movie. Only this wasn't a movie. This was my life. At least this was what was left of my life.

"Piece of shit needs to shift."

"Alpha said to leave him alone, Rance."

"Well, Alpha ain't here, and I'm going to teach this trash a lesson."

Oh, how I wished Alpha was here. He was the only bright spot of this entire experience. Rance kicked me once more and slammed a hand down on top of my head. My teeth clanked together from the force of it. I cowered, trying to make myself as small as possible—so much for fighting back—my pain almost as great as my fear. This was the end. Rance wasn't going to wait for the Alpha to return. He was going to dispose of me himself.

"Stop!" the other man shouted.

I peeked an eye open to see the other man pushing Rance away.

Rance wasn't ready to stop.

I was going to die, and from the looks of things, it would be a slow and agonizing death. All because, what, I decided to go for a walk on the wrong day and everything went to hell?

My eyes blurred, tears filling them at the loss of everything I never had. My life had already been shitty, the hope of what was next what kept me going. Get into a good school, get a good job, get married, have two-point-five kids that I loved with all my heart and would never abandon, grow old surrounded by grandbabies—that had been my plan. Now, breathing another day was all I could hope for.

The door cracked again, and I drew up my knees, waiting for the worst, and then the scent of the room changed, and my fear slowly started to evaporate. Cognitively, I knew I was still going to die. Of course I was. Those vile men would see to it. But right now, I felt safe. I lowered my knees as some kind of sick sign of my trust, covering my cock with my hands to be somewhat respectful.

I seemed to blackout for a moment, and the next thing I knew, I was alone with the two men who looked alike. Twins, maybe? No—twins definitely. One of them was Alpha, and I hadn't caught the other's name.

"Can you stand?" Alpha said, and I nodded in what I

thought to be the truth. I wasn't entirely sure. He looked back and forth between me and his brother. "Will you please stand?"

It took a bit, but I rose to my feet, my legs not doing okay. Not at all. I was still naked, and though I had bigger problems to worry about, modesty still won, and I covered myself with my hands. Nakedness didn't seem to faze these people, but I wasn't used to it.

Was this some sort of nudist colony that also transformed into wolves?

The nice one stepped closer to me; he sniffed the air between us, and I couldn't help but catch his scent. I noticed scents so much more now since my own wolf had been…unlocked? Set free? Invaded? Whatever. He smelled like safety and security. Like a warm blanket fresh from the laundry.

"Okay, Alpha." I leaned against the wall and allowed myself to slide back down.

"I was wrong? You're not a new wolf?" he asked, tilting his head in confusion.

"He's asking if you have worn your fur before or just skin," the other clarified, his hand still firmly on Alpha's shoulder. It wasn't a move of comfort from where I was sitting. No, it was a control thing. But control him from what? Surely, he wasn't going to hurt me.

"First time." Or second. How many times had I shifted now? They all blurred together.

"And you call him Alpha?" he asked, his eyes narrowed.

That one didn't trust me, but he wasn't about to kill me like the other asshat.

"It's his name, right?"

"No, little wolf. It is my job, my title." His voice softened as if I were fragile. Shit. I was fragile. I couldn't even stand enough to have a conversation.

"Oh." I mean, what else was there to say to that? "I'm Cord."

"I'm Byrom, and this is my twin and Beta, Lyle."

Byrom. That name fit him so much better.

"What were you doing in our territory? Didn't anyone teach you that it was dangerous?"

"I was just walking in the woods, and my boots were tight, so I took them off, and then next thing I knew, I was a wolf and watching from the inside, and then I saw you and the others, and you know the rest."

"You didn't realize you were about to gain your wolf?" Byrom's eyes never left mine. Gain? Had I lost him? What did that even mean?

"I didn't even know that people could do that—become animals—and next thing I knew, I was told I would die, was thrown in here, beaten until I couldn't breathe, and then here you are." A growl grew in his chest at my words, and I brought my knees back up. "Sorry," I mumbled, unsure what else to say, so I rambled. "That Rance guy came in with another guy, and I couldn't see what was coming from where after the first kick. That other guy stopped him, though. I'm not lying. I swear it, I'm not."

"You're scaring him, brother. He doesn't know our ways." Lyle now had two hands on the alpha, one on each shoulder. The alpha…not the name Alpha. I couldn't get anything right. "Cord, did your parents not tell you of the ways of the wolf?"

"I didn't have parents. I mean, I had foster parents…lots of them over the years, but no parents. They never said what happened to them. They said I was abandoned, but I don't believe that. Who does that to a child? When I was little, I used to pretend that they stumbled into the land of fae and just haven't been able to get back yet because fae time is different." I was rambling. Why was I telling him so much? I was slated to die, I'd already been beaten, and I was buck-ass naked, spilling my story to strangers, a story I never told anyone.

"Up," was all Byrom said, and I obeyed not out of fear, but this odd desire to please him. "You're coming home with me. You are not to run. Is that understood? If you do, you will die, and there will be nothing I can do about it."

"Alpha." Byrom shrugged off the man's hands at that one word.

"If you speak, know there will be consequences," he snipped and held out his hand for me, lowering his voice as he said, "I will help you. It's not far, and if we are lucky, no one will see us."

At least this one time I was lucky.

Chapter Eight

Byrom

Orphan.

Abandoned at birth.

Never knew his parents.

What kind of wolf, what kind of pack, would allow that to happen to a pup? My heart broke for him. The omega I had staying in my home, Cord, was beautiful, passionate, and sexy as all hell. That much I could tell already, and I'd only had him in my house for a few hours.

Cord Smith, a last name that had to have been simply assigned to him, not actually his real name. He was practically untraceable. How would we ever be able to determine where he came from and find his family? Would he even want that?

It was a topic I would have to discuss with him soon.

I sent a text to Lyle to have him round up the pack for a meeting. It would be tough, and my first decision as pack Alpha that deviated from the ways of our past, but I would do it. For Cord.

As I stepped outside my house, the bell calling the pack to our meeting space rang out. We had an area just outside the main house that served as our gathering space. It didn't have a podium or anything official, just a platform I could stand on to be heard and seen by all. This was where we had our pack meetings, and it was also where we began our runs.

Less than twenty-four hours earlier, we'd started a run, the run that brought us Cord. So much had changed in the blink of an eye. My pack needed reassurance and to know their Alpha had everything under control even if it looked different than they anticipated. Laws were there for a reason, but so was wisdom, and in this case, wisdom overshadowed the laws. I had faith that my pack would understand, with the exception of Rance, who would never be satisfied.

I couldn't ignore the issue of Rance anymore. He was more than the thorn in my side he'd always been. Now he was an outright challenger, my attempts to bring him to my side to somehow smooth things out not even beginning to show signs of working. I'd have to take care of him, and soon.

I stood on the platform for all to see, the eyes of those present now glued to me expectantly. Lyle came and stood by my side, as he always did. There was power in the two of us, sharing a face and similar in strength standing side by side in solidarity. Why Father had once thought it was a good idea to separate us and have Lyle eventually leave our pack was beyond me. He had been in talks with the Ashcliff pack about an arranged mating between their son and Lyle, but since his passing, the

Ashcliff pack hadn't mentioned the topic. Lyle was a hard pass on that idea anyway. We were stronger together. Full stop.

The pack continued to gather, curiosity on their faces, and few whispers between them. There had been rumors, rumors no doubt fueled by Rance. The other Betas would respect the implied confidentiality until I addressed the pack.

"I know you are all curious about the wolf we found in the woods and what he was doing there. Mostly, I am sure you are concerned if he's a threat to us and what I'm going to do about it. Protocol dictates that if no pack claims him and gives a sound reason as to why he would be trespassing on our land, we're to end him. I'm here to tell you now that that will not be happening."

Murmurs fluttered through the crowd like a wave, but no one seemed overly surprised or upset about it. I couldn't recall a time when we'd had to invoke that rule anyway. I knew my grandfather had when he was Alpha, but those were the old days when packs were less civilized. These days, we all kept to ourselves.

Rance, who should have been standing at Lyle's side as one of my Betas, snorted from his position in the back of the crowd.

"Cord is a wolf, orphaned at birth, raised in the human foster care system," I continued. "He was never told of his heritage. He is of no threat to us."

"You believe him?" Laurence called out from the crowd. His voice was curious but not skeptical. As a father of young pups, I understood his concern.

“I do. Absolutely. If anyone has concerns about this decision, please bring them up to me. I would be happy to discuss them. But this decision is final. Cord will be staying here, in the packhouse with me. I would like the pack to welcome him with open arms and teach him our ways. He needs to learn to be a wolf.”

“What if he decides he doesn’t want to be a part of a pack? He’s lived as a human his whole life,” another person asked.

I swallowed thickly, and my heartbeat kicked up a notch. My wolf paced within me. That simply wouldn’t be allowed to happen. “He won’t,” I said finally, hoping that what I had said was true.

“Why do you care so much for this lone wolf? Is he your mate or something?” Rance had the audacity to speak out. Of all the pack members, he was the only exhibiting any trepidation at welcoming Cord to the pack.

I growled. “Do you have something you want to say, Rance? A challenge you want to issue? Or are you just going to keep pussyfooting around it like a coward?” Perhaps my vow of not executing anyone today would prove to be false. I would gladly take Rance down. My wolf would relish it.

He snorted but said no more. He wouldn’t issue a direct challenge. If he had the balls to go after me, he would have done so already. He let out a low whimper, his wolf recognizing the stronger alpha that I was. The pack snickered.

I addressed the pack, tearing my gaze from Rance. "You all know my open-door policy. Talk to me if you have any concerns. If you want to talk with one of my Betas, they will listen as well. But Cord stays. That's my final decision."

"Yes, Alpha," Mia, our pack schoolteacher, said from the front row, followed by several more murmurs of the same.

I stepped down from the podium and began the trek back to my home. Mia stopped me along the way.

"Let me know if there's anything I can do for the young man. Growing up in such a way must have been terrible, and then to find out that he's a wolf to boot? He's got to be traumatized."

"Thank you," I said, my heart warming and pride swelling within me. "I appreciate it."

My pack was good and kind. We'd make sure Cord was safe. We'd make sure he was accepted. Rance was an anomaly, not the norm.

"The rest of the pack will lose any trepidation with time. In the meanwhile, take good care of him. Especially if he is your mate." She winked. Was I that obvious or was she just that in tune? I had a feeling it was a little bit of both.

I smiled. "That isn't for certain." Though I was beginning to suspect it was true.

She grinned. "Only one way to find out. We will have a welcome party for him at the next new moon, when he is more settled."

"Thank you," I said. "That would be wonderful."

I walked back to my home quickly. While I was making plans with the pack, Cord was at my home terrified of his fate. He had no idea what pack life was like, what it meant to be a wolf. For all he knew, most of the alphas were like Rance in their less-than-welcoming embrace.

Mate. Claim.

That wouldn't be happening, at least not yet. I kept my wolf in check. If it were up to him, we'd have claimed Cord already. Sometimes I wondered if life would be easier if I just let my wolf take lead. And it probably would be, but it would also be bloodier, and that wasn't a fair trade.

When I stepped inside my house, I wasn't alone. Cord was there, obviously. His soft snores came from the couch, but there was another person as well, putting my wolf on edge.

Protect. My wolf needed to calm down. It was Lissy, and out of all people, she was the one Cord least likely needed protection from.

"Lissy?" I tiptoed to the kitchen, careful not to wake Cord from his well-deserved rest.

"I'm here," she answered back. She was just putting the kettle on when I stepped into the room.

"Well, you've had an exciting day," she said.

Lissy was my cousin and our pack healer. She'd gone to college for nursing, with a minor in animal science. An odd combination for a nursing student, but it made total sense to a wolf shifter. Her omega father had also been a pack healer. It was in her blood.

"It's been…something," I confessed. Out of the entire pack, my full trust went to one person—Lyle. But after him, a close second was Lissy.

"Is he your mate? Lyle thinks he is your mate." Maybe she had more of my trust than Lyle.

"Gossip much?" I groaned, oddly relieved he had brought it up with her. I needed to process this all. "I don't know. He can't be, can he? I mean, I'm the Alpha. I should have a…" A what? A real wolf? Cord was a real wolf; he just had no idea about any of this. "Right now, I just want to be his friend and to help him get back on his feet."

She eyed me cautiously. "Mmhmm. When he gets up, make sure he drinks two cups of the tea I am brewing. That boy looks a little underfed, and shifting takes its toll on a body."

Feed. Provide. Mate.

"Thanks, Lissy. Let me know if you hear any chatter from the pack, please." I didn't need to explain to her what kind of chatter I meant.

"Yes, Alpha. I'll be attending to the omegas in the dorm first thing tomorrow. If there is gossip, they'll fill me in." Nothing fueled gossip like a dorm full of single wolves.

"Thanks."

Chapter Nine

Cord

"I'm going to be fired." If I hadn't been already. There was no way the bar was taking me back—that was for sure—and Adrianne might be able to cover my ass at the office, but the chances were good she wouldn't risk it. We might be friendly or possibly even friends, but she had a decent job with benefits and wasn't going to risk that for my per diem ass.

"Your life is here." Just like Byrom. No fancy words or fluffy sentiments. Right to the point. I kind of liked it. No. There was no kinda to it. I loved it.

"My bills are there." I sighed, leaning back in my seat, poking my eggs with my fork. I'd been here for over a week, and even though I knew I was basically a prisoner, no bone in my body wanted to leave. Sure, my bills and job and such called to me because all my life I'd been told to be a responsible adult, which meant a grown-up job with grown-up bills, but staying there? Nope. I belonged here, as weird as that was.

"Give them to me." He downed his coffee. "I will deal with them."

“That’s not really how life works, and besides, these aren’t just my cable bill.” Not that I’d had the luxury of cable or internet aside from my prepaid cell phone in goodness knew how long. “I have an overdue electric bill, rent, and more student loans than should be legal. I can’t just give them to you.”

“Why not?” He cocked his head to the side, his brow furrowed as if it perplexed him why I couldn’t just hand over all my bills and problems to him.

“I can’t, and I’m not going to just because you tell me I have to.” When I first came to his home, I’d have never spoken to him like that. Shit, I was scared to speak to him period. My body was a crumpled mess, my fear high with all the execution talk, and quite frankly, the fact that he was a wolf part of the time scared the shit out of me.

And yeah, that was weird coming from someone who did the same, but at the time, I sort of thought it was a dream or a fluke or something. But nope. It was my new life. I was hairy as could be some of the time. Un-freaking-believable.

“No one talks to me that way.” He set his fork on the table, his tone one of amusement, not anger. “At least not without being reminded of their place.” He stood up, taking his dishes with him. “Do you know your place, little wolf?”

“Apparently, it’s here.” I was being a brat, but I didn’t even care.

“It is. Now give me your bills.” He stepped to the sink and deposited his dishes in there. “Cord.”

“I need to go back to my place.” Not really for the bills. I could pull them up on my phone, which by some miracle survived all of this. Lyle, Cord’s brother, who looked freakily like him minus an inch on his height, had also saved my boots. He was a good guy. I wasn’t so sure about the rest of them.

Well, Rance I was sure of; that guy was a piece of shit and didn’t respect Byrom. Crap. Wasn’t that the same exact thing I was doing?

“If you take me to my place, we can get the bills and things, and maybe if it’s not too much trouble, we can square things with my landlord.” That last part hurt to admit.

“Eat, little wolf. And then we will take care of everything.” We. Not I, as if he were my savior, even though he sort of was. If Rance had been in charge, they’d have killed me already. He made that quite clear.

I ate the rest of my eggs. Byrom made sure I had plenty of protein at each meal, and leaving any on the plate would have him reminding me about how my wolf required sustenance and blah blah blah. It was kind of nice to have someone care about my nutrition for the first time in…ever.

I put on my boots. This was okay. I could do this. I could trust him to help—at least with this. It wasn’t like foster care where they were pretending to care because they got a paycheck. Quite the opposite. He was about to lose a ton of money because of me, and he seemed almost happy about it. Weird.

He drove me to my place without having to ask for directions, all of the truck windows left wide open. I wanted to ask him how he knew my address, but at the same time, maybe it was best if I didn't. This whole pack thing still made little sense to me, and I had a feeling it was all connected.

"If there are things you want that don't fit in my truck, arrangements can be made." He had to practically shout for me to be able to hear.

"Is the AC broken?" If he couldn't afford to fix his truck's AC, he was going to pass the fuck out at the sight of my student loan balances.

"No."

"Can I?" I put my hand on the knob.

"No."

I dropped my hand, accidentally brushing his thigh with my hand. The touch brought on an immediate reaction from me. My dick hardened, my wolf howled, and my whole body grew hot.

Mine.

"Your wolf is close." He turned my corner and put the truck in park. "You need to let him out more."

No. What I needed to do was not touch the sexy man who made my wolf a possessive weirdo.

"I don't know how." I opened the truck door and jumped out, closing it a bit too forcefully and adjusting my shirt so Byrom didn't see my stupid erection.

We gathered my few personal possessions from my apartment, leaving the furniture and kitchenware for later. That was when the moment of truth came: the reason we were there. I slid open my kitchen drawer of shame where all bills wound up. Embarrassing was an understatement as he looked through them one by one. I should've gone paperless like they asked me to every month. At least then I wouldn't have to watch him as he saw all my inadequacies.

"And the others." He looked up at me, his *don't even try to lie to me* look perfected.

"My phone is prepaid, and the rent I just take to the management office. It's not a paper bill."

"And that is all?" How could he say that after looking at all that red?

"Yeah." I dropped my eyes to the ground, not wanting to see his disapproval, and to my surprise, he set them on the counter and went to the fridge, opened it up, closed it—then did the same with each of the cabinets. "Do you keep food elsewhere?"

"No."

"And you lived like this?"

"Fuck you!" The anger welled up inside me. It was bad enough to show him my faults, but to then have him judge me for them when I trusted him…just, no. "I did the best I could. I worked…a lot, and I never got sent to collections. I was just sometimes close to that. I'm not a deadbeat. I'm just doing the best I can." I would not cry. I would not cry. I would not cry. I would not cry.

Footsteps echoed as I willed my tears away. And then arms, warm arms, wrapped around me. Byrom was…hugging me. Great, now I was crying.

"You survived…without a pack. No one should have to do that. No. One." He squeezed me close, his scent calming me. I wasn't sure exactly what all was going on, and at that moment, I didn't care. I just wanted to stay there in his arms.

"Let's go teach your wolf how to come out." He stepped away from me, back to his direct and official self. "I'll take care of these, but I need you to direct me to the management office."

"Yeah. Okay." I wiped the tears from my cheeks as nonchalantly as I could. "It's across the parking lot."

We went in, and Byrom just wrote a check. Just like that. He didn't even blink at the numbers.

"Let's go." He walked past me and out to the truck. I climbed inside, and just as before, he had the windows wide open.

We drove in silence most of the way until I couldn't take it anymore. "I'll pay you back or work for it or something. I need a job."

"You will have a job, and you will contribute to the pack. It's what pack does. But first you need to gain control of your wolf. It's not safe for you to be among humans until you do."

“I lived among humans my whole life,” I counter-argued. “And besides, I can’t bring him out even when I try. The only time I have is when I’m forced to, and I’m not even sure how that works.”

“Your wolf wasn’t awake then. Things are different now. I can scent him so close to the surface.”

“Then teach me.” I rolled up my window because screw that. “Roll yours up, please.”

“You’ll be sorry.” He smirked as he rolled his up. I had no idea what he was talking about at first. Less than a minute later, I did, my jeans too tight and my desire to touch him overwhelmingly strong.

Sure, I’d been attracted to him. Who wouldn’t be? He was hot, protective, and kind in his own rough-around-the-edges kind of way. And the way he wore his jeans…I dared anyone not to feel something at the sight of that. And hard-ons had been commonplace—of course they were.

But this—this feeling as we sat there in his truck, windows closed, recirculating air blowing in our face, went so far beyond that. I wanted to beg him to pull over so I could climb on his lap. I wanted to slip my hand under his shirt to feel the plane of his abs. I wanted to—mine.

Stupid wolf was right. I wanted to make him mine. I wanted my scent mixed with his in a way that left no question about who Byrom belonged to.

I had those windows down so fast, Byrom’s rich laughter

filling the air.

"What the fuck was that?" I squirmed in my seat, placing my hands over the bulge in my pants.

"That was your wolf wanting to come out to play. Let's help him along." He was talking in riddles, but as he pulled into the clearing and turned off the engine, I saw how serious he was about helping me shift—the rest of the crazy *want to jump him* bit aside.

"Get naked." Maybe not completely aside. He pulled off his shirt and threw it in the truck's window, which was still open, and toed off his shoes. "Hurry up now. You don't want to ruin your boots, do you?" Damn him for seeing their value.

I took them off and set them on my seat and took off my shirt. Byrom already stood there naked, his full cock just waving in the air. I squeezed my eyes tight.

"Don't like what you see?" he teased. "Get your jeans off. Let's run."

"I don't know how."

"Which is why we are here. Hurry along now." I removed the last of my clothing and walked around to stand where I could see him better, not to look, but to, you know, learn—and look. Cause, fine, he was worth looking at. I put my hands in front of me. I didn't get the whole *it's fine to be naked* thing, and even if I did, having him see how he affected me wasn't ideal.

"You need to get rid of that human thinking if we are going to make this work." He pointed to my hands.

"Let's try it anyway." I wasn't ready to show him my junk—not when it gave so much away. My hands barely covered me, especially since my dick was not behaving.

"If you say so. Close your eyes and talk to your wolf."

I closed my eyes. "What do I say?"

"It doesn't matter. Just let him know you know he's there and that you don't hate him." My eyes popped open.

"I never said I hated him," I insisted. Scared of him for a bit? Sure. Confused by him? Heck, yeah. Scared? No. Not really. "I just don't understand him."

"Then tell him that."

"Fine." I slammed my eyes closed again. *Wolf. Wolf. I'm here. Are you here? I don't hate you. Byrom says you think I do, but I don't. I promise.*

Nothing. He didn't reply back, didn't do that grumble thing he'd been doing lately, didn't so much as peek his head up.

"It didn't work."

"It wasn't meant to have you shift, little wolf. It was to get you ready to shift." Great, I was standing there talking to myself because…why? I needed to feel better about myself?

A part of me, anyway. That was when it clicked for the first time. My wolf was part of me. I wasn't a weird host or something. He was me and I was him.

"You talk in riddles." Why couldn't he have just said what I needed to learn? Then maybe I wouldn't still be standing here cupping myself.

"I allow you much leeway with me, but do me a favor and don't speak to me like that in front of others."

"They'll get mad?"

"No. They will demand I punish you." My body stiffened at the thought of that. My original punishment was meant to be death, and that was simply for being in the wrong place. What would punishment over disrespecting an Alpha be? Not that I was really disrespecting him, but I was being fresh, as my third foster mother called it when she threw me back into the system.

"Now that we have that clear, close your eyes again, only this time when you talk to your wolf, ask him to come out to play. Ask him to run."

"It's easier when you tell him." Then he just did it even if I didn't want him to. He listened to Byrom. "Is that because you're an alpha or the Alpha or whatever?"

"Yes and no. We can talk about pack dynamics later. First, let's get you to shift. I won't always be there when you need your wolf."

I closed my eyes. *Run. Let's run.*

Nothing.

It's time to play, little wolf, I tried the words Byrom sometimes used.

Nothing.

Please. I want to run.

"Tell him," Byrom spoke more forcefully.

"I am," I whispered. "I am."

Please, come out. Byrom wants us to run. Something clicked this time, and I felt him rising up.

Mate. Mine. Run. He repeated it over and over again as my bones started to crack, this shift far less painful than any before it. When I opened my eyes, I was on all four paws, and Byrom's wolf stood in front of me for only a second before he took off like a shot.

I ran after him, my mind still on the forefront, unlike the first time I shifted. I ran as fast as my feet could go, and as I closed in on him, the first and only thing I could think to do was to pounce, so pounce I did, landing on him and knocking him to the ground, rolling us both over.

Fast little wolf. How was he talking to me?

He rolled us over again and jumped back, shifting as he did.

I wanted to join him and thought back to what he said. *I want to stand on two.* The words were hardly coherent, but he understood, and I found myself on my hands and knees wearing no fur, only skin. Not an ache, pain, or crack.

"Whoa."

Byrom's hand came down, and I took it, allowing him to help me up. "I…we…the wolf and I, we did it."

"Yes, little wolf, you did it, and you're fast. Like scary fast. No one catches up to me. No one." He sounded almost proud. No. Not almost. He was proud—of me—of my wolf.

"I did." And without thinking, I threw my arms around him, going in for a hug, and part way through it my lips acted on their own accord, slamming into Byrom's, needing to feel him, taste him, explore him.

His hand came behind my head, his fingers threaded through my hair as he deepened the kiss. It was bliss until…until he pulled back. His eyes held a pain in them that I hadn't noticed before, and I reached up to cup his cheek. He jumped back, shifting midair and running back to the truck.

Fuck.

We need to follow him, I instructed my wolf.

At least my wolf didn't argue with me, and we were on all fours reaching the truck just as he climbed in. My clothes were on the grass outside the passenger side door, waiting for me.

Byrom spent the rest of our day together pretending the kiss never happened and acting all hot shifter professor, explaining the ins and outs of pack life. Not that I heard most of it. My mind was still one hundred percent focused on that kiss, even after he left for a meeting that night.

Gah. Why did I have to kiss him? And worse, why did I long to do it again and again and again?

Chapter Ten

Byrom

Ignore it. Don't think about it.

It didn't even happen.

That was my mantra for each and every passing day that I spent with Cord. I didn't allow myself to look at him for too long for fear that my heart would ache with longing and my face would show just how much my wolf wanted him. If I thought about him for too long, my face would split into a goofy grin, because Cord made me happy.

I knew because Lissy had caught me thinking about Cord while he was learning how to control his tail in his wolf form. The whole lesson had been hilarious and adorable. I still laughed when I thought about it. She had pointed out just how goofy I looked smiling to myself, just this side of teasing. Had it been anyone else, I might've cared—but with her, that was a guard I'd willingly let down.

I most certainly never thought about the kiss.

Except I spent so much time reminding myself not to think about it that it was all I thought about.

Cord was off limits, at least for now. He had to be. The man was recovering from his past, recovering from the trauma of being captured by wolves and having his life turned upside down. He'd recently learned that his life was completely different than he ever thought it was.

I was trying to be the best Alpha I could for my pack, while also trying to determine what to do with Rance. He'd been oddly accommodating and calm since I'd taken Cord in, and that worried me. If it was one thing you could count on Rance to be, it was a pain in the ass.

Cord took to being a wolf naturally. His shifts came quicker and quicker with each passing day. But still, something stopped him from embracing his wolf completely. He still had to remind himself to listen to his wolf's instincts.

We stood in the kitchen, where he deliberately kept his pace slow as he cleaned up our breakfast dishes. It wasn't something I'd ever asked him to do; he just always took care of things, insisting he enjoyed it.

Apprehension flowed off of him in waves. I probably shouldn't have mentioned what today's lesson would be about. He was dragging his feet, and given he grew up human, understandably so.

"Do I really have to learn all this?" he asked me after I'd grabbed his hand and gently pulled him outside, wanting to calm him with my touch while at the same time lighting a fire under his ass. The more he dawdled, the more apprehensive he would become, making the lesson exponentially harder.

The two of us stood in the yard behind the packhouse where we were out of view from other members of the pack. Eventually, they would stop and look in on us. They usually did when we did these types of training. The wolves of my pack were nothing if not nosy.

Cord and I hadn't gone back to the clearing where I'd originally taught him to shift. I wasn't asking for trouble. This semi-privacy would suit us nicely.

Most of the pack had kind words for Cord when they encountered him, but there was still an awkwardness to the encounters, and I didn't want to exacerbate that by letting them see what he would perceive as his weakness. He wanted everything to come quickly, and it did. Just not as instantaneously as he would've preferred.

"Part of being a wolf is giving in to some of our more basic instincts. We establish our dominance through fighting. Light sparring, most of the time, but sometimes it can get quite serious." I didn't elaborate on what that looked like, how our wolves longed for blood when true dominance was needed, how they wouldn't think twice about putting a wolf down who needed it. He would learn all of that soon enough. "I'm sure you've noticed many pack members bare their neck to me in submission when the situation calls for it."

"It's a little barbaric, don't you think?" Cord asked. He had no idea.

I sighed. To a human mind, of course it was. But he was a wolf. He just hadn't fully accepted it yet. "Well, it works." I half shrugged. "It's what we are. Part of us are animals, and we respect that part of ourselves, and you should, too."

Cord rolled his eyes, a move that would get any other wolf a serious growl from me, until they submitted as they should. But this was Cord, and I was patient with him. Plus, I kind of liked it. He didn't look at me as someone he needed to fear, and that somehow made all of our interactions deeper.

"I do," he said. "I respect my wolf; I respect your wolf very much." My wolf preened at the praise. "I just have never been much of a fighter. And I don't want to start now."

My heart went out to him. He was an omega thorough and through. Cord was meant to nurture and care, not fight. But I hated the idea of leaving him unprotected. And until he had an alpha, he needed to protect himself.

Ours.

My wolf wasn't wrong even if both the timing and the situation were.

"Let me just teach you a few of the basics." I could compromise. It wasn't a tactic I usually used, but with Cord I thought it could work.

"Okay." He nodded. "Sure. Whatever gets this over with quickly."

We ran through the basics at a slower pace. I wasn't about to let our lesson run short simply because we were cutting the curriculum in half. I wanted as much time with him as I could possibly get.

“Again,” I said when he worked on a punch for the fifteenth time.

“What are you gonna do when I actually hit you?” he asked with a smirk.

I chuckled. I’d sparred with many of the alphas in the pack as well as my Betas, and none of them had ever gotten the drop on me. “That’s never gonna happen.” He gave me the *sure, if you say so* look.

“Can we go inside now?” he said. “Our time is pretty much up.”

Damn, I was a sap when it came to him. I let him walk all over me. If he asked for the moon, I’d find a way to get it. Thank goodness the pack wasn’t around to see it. It reminded me a lot of how my alpha father had been with my omega dad, the Alpha Omega. “Yeah. You did well. Better than I—”

Cord’s fist flew quicker than I’d seen it. My eyes began to water as the pain radiated through my face.

My wolf howled within me, equal parts annoyed at being caught off guard and extremely proud of our omega for taking us by surprise.

“Wow,” I said. “You pack quite a punch.”

Cord had his hands over his mouth. “Oh my goodness, I didn’t expect that to actually work. I thought maybe, since you were a little distracted, but I didn’t mean to hurt you.”

I held up a hand. “I’m fine,” I said as I wrinkled my face,

trying to clear the tears from my eyes. "That was very good. You did great."

Cord's lips twitched like he wanted to smile, but he stopped himself. "Okay, but I don't think I ever want to do that again. Are you hurt?" Cord stepped closer to me and put a hand on my shoulder. He inspected my face, getting up on his tippy toes so he could see me clearly.

"I'm fine," I said. "I promise. That was impressive. No one's ever been able to do that."

"No kidding," Lyle said from the back deck. His shoulders shook with silent laughter. He and Lissy both stood there watching. She held a hand over her face to contain her laughter.

Great, both of them saw.

"You did so awesome, Cord! I've really never been happier to see somebody punch my brother like that," Lyle said.

Cord beamed, though his cheeks pinked from embarrassment. "I didn't mean to hurt him."

"I'm fine," I repeated. Though my nose hurt. I no longer doubted my omega could take care of himself should he ever need to. "Okay. Let's go inside."

Inside, Lissy had set the table, and Lyle was sitting, ready to dig into the steaks she had grilled for us. She had also brought over an array of dishes for us: a pan of macaroni and cheese, steamed green beans, grilled steaks, and even a pie.

“You spoil us, Lissy,” I said. And I wasn’t complaining. Lissy was by far the best cook in the pack, and she loved to spoil people with her meals.

“Well, we haven’t gotten a chance to have a family dinner in a while, so I wanted to do something.” She beamed as she put serving utensils with each dish.

I grimaced. “Thank you.”

“Is it because of me being here? Is that why you haven’t had your regular dinners?” Cord asked. He took the seat next to me. Most nights we ate at the breakfast nook in the kitchen or outdoors on the deck. Tonight was special and warranted the dining room. “I’m surprised you aren’t sitting at the head of the table. Seems like that’s where the Alpha would sit.”

I winced. He was right. The head of the table would make sense. Lissy, Lyle, and I all looked at the empty seat. It was where my alpha dad had sat each night for family dinners.

“Did I say something wrong?” He bit his bottom lip.

I put a hand on Cord’s shoulder and rubbed my thumb over the back of his neck. “No, little wolf. It’s just…that’s my dad’s chair, and I—” couldn’t bring myself to take his spot.

“You haven’t told him about…” Lissy trailed off.

I shook my head. “I didn’t get a chance.” I turned to face Cord. “I haven’t always been the Alpha. Up until last month, I was just an Alpha-in-training, the heir apparent by title. My father was the Alpha. The title was to be passed on to me when my father was ready to retire, but he…he died suddenly in an accident." I wasn't sure why I hadn't mentioned it before. No. That was a lie. I didn't say anything because the wound was too raw.

Cord sucked in a breath and grabbed my hand. "I'm sorry, Byrom. I didn't know."

"It's okay. I should have told you by now. He was on his way home from a meeting with another pack. He had his Betas and my omega father with him. They all passed." An entire generation of leadership gone in an instant. "Since then, the pack has been in mourning. Not only did we lose our Alpha, but all of our highest leaders."

"It must be so hard for you, to deal with the loss of your parents while taking on this role." Cord's hand trailed up my arm, comforting me with his touch. My wolf practically purred.

"I'm fine. It is the pack I worry about." I lied. I wasn't fine. Lyle wasn't, either. But we were getting there.

"You're a good leader. Your father taught you well." He gave my shoulder a squeeze. "But allowing yourself and the pack time to grieve is important."

I leaned into his touch. He was right. How he managed to say all the right things, I'd never know.

"I think it's time we gave the pack a reason to celebrate," Lissy said, her grin wide. I knew what she implied. She wanted me to claim Cord as my mate. Which I wanted as well, but he needed to be ready. I needed to be ready.

"That sounds like a great idea!" Lyle agreed.

"Let's dig in. Dinner's getting cold." I turned back to the table and reached for a steak.

Chapter Eleven

Cord

"Are you sure you are up for tonight? No pressure," Lyle asked as he came to fetch me for the first pack run since I'd arrived. Byrom left an hour earlier to do a perimeter run with Gio and left me alone to allow my nerves to grow.

This was huge. I could feel it. It was one thing for the pack to be nice to me because Byrom basically told them to. It was another for their wolves to accept mine.

"I need to." And Byrom needed me to. Now that I understood how new the whole Alpha thing was to him and the horrific catalyst for him gaining the position, I had a better understanding of the tightrope he was currently walking.

"If you are sure." Lyle headed out the door, stopping midway. "Just know that you are safe. My brother would die to assure it, and I would be by his side."

I opened my mouth to say something…anything, but he was out the door and down the steps before a single word came to me. Byrom would die for me. Lyle would die for his brother even if it was to defend me. How did I deserve this loyalty?

I didn't.

But at the same time, I felt the same way. Like this need for Byrom to be okay. No, better than okay. Thriving. I needed him to live his best life. It was weird yet somehow not.

I scurried to catch up to Lyle, and we walked in silence to the clearing where the pack had their runs. Byrom was already on the platform, and most everyone I had met or seen in passing was already there, many of whom were mostly if not completely naked.

"Was I supposed to be naked?" I asked Lyle as we walked around the gathering and to the platform.

"Not yet." He pointed to a spot, which I took to mean where I was to stand, and I immediately took it. I must've understood his intent because he gave me a nod and joined his brother on the platform, the other Betas all joining him as well.

"Brother and Sister wolves, tonight we will run as a pack in celebration of our newest wolves. This month, we have had four new shifts within our pack. There is much to celebrate." He called up three young boys and one young girl up to the stage. All of us clapped, with a few whistles mixed in.

"It is not until our first shifts that we truly become in tune with our wolves—it is then that we finally become whole. Lacy, Casper, Troy, and Zander, tonight we celebrate you and the amazing young men and woman you are becoming. It would be our honor to have you start our run when it is time."

One by one, they bared their necks and said, "Yes, Alpha. If the pack will have me."

"Then so be it." Byrom stood to their side, and the gathering cheered once more.

"This evening brings us one more wolf, a wolf who shifted for the first time exactly one month ago, a wolf raised with no pack, a wolf who we would be honored to call ours. Cord, please join us." The young wolves took a huge step back, the small platform extremely crowded.

It took me a few seconds to process what he was asking, but then I joined him there, in front of everyone. It was one thing to feel like they accepted me, but this…this would let me know for sure. And other than a little side eye from Rance, not one face I saw held anything other than a smile.

"Tonight will be Cord's first official run with us, as well. But unlike our young, Cord is joining us in more ways than one, for tonight we welcome him into our pack."

Wait? What? I mean, yeah, sure, I wanted it but also really? Why hadn't they told me?

"Take off your shirt," Lyle whispered, and his earlier comments started to make sense. In his own weird way, he was preparing me for this.

I took off my shirt and held it in front of me in a ball.

"Cord, kneel." I dropped to my knees, but not in the way

I'd been dreaming about. No. They went thud on the wooden platform, facing the pack.

"The Greycoast Pack has a long history of strength, courage, and honor. Only wolves who possess such traits are accepted into the fold at their age of maturity, or in Cord's case, tonight. Cord kneels here tonight as an omega who exemplifies these traits." He then hopped off the stage, stood in front of me, and bared his neck. One by one, his Betas did, Rance the only one who partially shifted his hand first, glaring at me. I wasn't sure what the fuck that even meant. Relief flooded me as he stepped to the side. This continued until every person in the clearing had stood in front of me, tipping their head to the side and then shucking their clothing.

"Our pack has welcomed you, Cord. Please join us on our run." The four young shifters shifted. They didn't have the grace that Byrom had, and it took a bit longer for Casper than the others, but once they had all shifted, they loped off, the rest of the group shifting and joining them as I was still shucking my jeans, Byrom at my side.

"Hurry up, little wolf. It's time to run," he teased.

"You didn't tell me."

"If I did, you would worry about the results." He took me by the hand. "Now let's run."

"Results?" I wasn't going to be told something like that to just let it go unelaborated. He should know me well enough to know that by now.

"If a pack member doesn't accept you into the fold, they

claw you as a physical sign."

Holy shit. That was the threat in Rance's eyes. Gods, I hated his sorry ass. "Now let's run." He stepped forward, taking his fur as he did. It took me a bit longer, but I soon joined him, running in the direction of the pack.

Only a few feet into the woods, I was pounced on by one of the cubs that was on the run—then another and another and another.

Have fun, Cord. Byrom chuckled in my mind and took off to who knew where.

The cubs and I pounced, ran, climbed, and even took a few leaps into the water. It was one thing to have the adults accept me by not making me bleed, even if that was exactly what Rance had wanted to do, but this…this was true acceptance. The youth of the pack accepted me as their own. I didn't know if it was because they sensed my wolf was, in many ways, as young as theirs or if it was because of the times I sat in on their classes trying to learn the way of things. In the end, it didn't matter. They accepted me. I was part of their pack.

I belonged, for the first time in my life. I belonged somewhere. What could be better than that?

Chapter Twelve

Byrom

My heart filled with so much joy, watching the pack young ambush Cord the way they did. They waited for him not because they had to. No, they waited because they wanted to. He was theirs.

I bound off as they all played, stopping to look behind me a few times, wondering if he would be as playful with our young and stopping myself right there. This was not the time for those thoughts. We needed to get him adjusted to pack life before throwing the whole mate thing at him.

I found my brother and Betas, and we hunted a stag. It had been a long time since we hunted together, and consequently, we almost lost the beast a couple of times due to our lack of practice and Rance trying to take over and go in for the kill too early.

In the end, victory was ours. We circled the stag until he became disoriented then slowly pushed him towards the clearing. My brother and I took him down, showing our power as well as our ability to work together. Historically, that was huge. For us, not so much. I never understood the brother versus brother power struggle. But then again, Lyle was my brother and closest friend. I'd gladly abdicate for him. Not that he wanted it.

Shit. Neither of us did, yet here we were. Maybe that was what had Rance's underwear in a bunch. He wanted power—craved it, even. For me to have and not want what he desired more than anything and to have it go to someone who might not want it—I could see his point. Not that it excused his actions.

He might've thought he was being sly during the ceremony, but his little claw threat didn't go unnoticed.

We dragged our kill the short distance to the clearing where we would share our bounty with the pack, another way to celebrate the new wolves and in a way honor those we had lost but upholding our traditions.

I howled calling the pack home. The wolves came back in pairs or small groups, stopping at the stag briefly then moving to the platform, where they shifted back to their human form, not bothering with their clothing. There was a feast tonight, a feast that required teeth.

"Brother and Sister Wolves, tonight we feast as a pack. It is with mourning hearts that this feast is brought to us by new leadership, our late Alpha and Betas torn from us too soon. But they are not gone. No. They live in each and every one of us. Their indelible mark is seen everywhere, from the new wolves who led us on our run to the way we welcomed a new pack member. They are here with us in here," I pointed to my head, "and in here," and placed my hand on my heart. "Let us honor them by remembering our past and learning from it, both the good and the bad, as we forged our future."

My brother flanked my right side, and the other Betas joined him, taking his lead.

"Thank you, brothers, for helping to provide for our pack. You gifted us with food, but also with your wisdom, strength, and commitment."

I nodded to the pack, who came up one at a time, bared their necks, then shifted. One by one, they thanked us for our service with their sign of submission. I'd seen it done a thousand times growing up and was on the other side for most of those times. Never had I felt the power of the simple gesture before. They trusted me, trusted us, and were willing to give us the power to continue our task.

My father used to say it was a weak Alpha who took his power. I never understood it before that moment. I didn't earn or deserve this position. I always knew that. But in my mind, my father gave it to me. How wrong I was. It was my father or my blood line or any of that. It was my pack who gave me the power—gave us the power.

And when the final wolf came up and bared his neck, Cord's eyes never leaving mine, the emotion of it nearly broke me. Here was a man who didn't grow up with our ways, a man who might never fully embrace them, a man who had every reason to not accept any of this, and he was giving me his submission as a packmate while showing me he would always think of me as just Byrom. It was almost too much, so I did what any wolf would and commanded my Betas to run, following closely behind them.

It was time to let our wolves take control. There would be time for human thoughts and feelings and discussions later. For now, my wolf needed to see our mate eat the food we provided.

I was no longer going to deny he was mine.

I just needed to hope that one day I would be his.

Chapter Thirteen

Cord

There was something about the whole sparring thing that just did it for me, at least in wolf form. While human, I still hated it and probably always would, but as a wolf…I now craved it. It wasn't all blood and danger like I first thought. It was more than that.

Once I got over the initial dislike of the fighting idea, I found that I enjoyed the playful side of sparring. I didn't understand it. I wasn't a violent person, not even close. Heck, I had a second grader punch me in the stomach my fifth-grade year, and I ran to tell the teacher—in tears. I hadn't been in a fight since, and I still flinched thinking about when I decked Byrom. I'd been so sure he'd stop me. I wasn't making that mistake again, even if Lyle begged me to on more than one occasion.

"Did you want to fight?" I nonchalantly asked Byrom as I poured myself a glass of water. "Not like for real or anything, but for, you know, fun?"

"Your wolf likes it, doesn't he?" He smirked.

No, my wolf liked Byrom. And so did I. And it sucked. I was a walking hard-on pretty much all of the time, either because he was near me and my body took that as a sign of all engines go or because he wasn't with me and I wanted him to be. It was getting to be a real problem.

"I guess?" I shrugged off, not wanting to show too much enthusiasm.

"My wolf does, too." He shucked his shirt, and all I wanted to do was run my fingers over the planes of his chest. Instead, I just placed my hand gently on his bare skin and let it set there, wanting more—needing more—but so unsure of everything.

After that kiss, he booked so fast and then played the *ignore it and it never happened* game. Not that I was any better about that. I never mentioned it, either. But in my case, it was more that I didn't want to hear the words of rejection from his mouth than anything else. It was official. I was a chicken. My wolf was just some sort of cloak.

But then the time to discuss it came and went. Bringing it up now would just be awkward and weird.

Hearing about his parents and feeling the turmoil he felt at their deaths, seeing him with his pack as they mourned their losses, watching him bring them all together during the run, his words so much deeper than I suspected even he knew—all of that solidified it for me: this was a man I wanted.

I wanted more kisses, and I wanted those everywhere, not just my lips. But there was the whole chicken in wolf's clothing dilemma.

Right now, though? Standing so close, our bodies connected, if only by a hand, the chicken went wobbling away. Or was that turkeys? It didn't matter. What mattered was the connection I felt.

He didn't move, emboldening me to take a step closer. "It's not just me, right? This attraction?" I asked with bravery I didn't know I had. And really, if left on my own, I didn't. Something about touching him, inhaling his scent, made me stronger. I needed it to be two sided; I needed it more than I needed my next breath.

"No." He took my hand, and at first, I thought it was to get me away from him—a signal my advances were unwelcome, yet again, but he just slowly moved my hand lower. My gods, he was harder than I was. How was that even possible?

"If you keep licking your lips like that, I'm going to find something better to do with them." As if that was a reason to stop.

"I can think of something better." I dropped to my knees, not thinking through the consequences—not even caring.

A low growl filled my ears, and I looked up, wondering if I had crossed a line. "You growled."

"No, Cord. I didn't." I looked up at him in confusion. "That was you." He chuckled.

I growled? Me. Ours. No. Not me. My wolf. Whoa.

He bent down and scooped me up. "You're hungry." He nipped my bottom lip. "And so am I." He was so not wrong on that. I nestled into him, loving the feeling of being in his arms as he held me close, carrying my weight as if I weighed nothing.

Byron jogged…jogged with me in his arms straight to his bedroom, not letting me down until we reached the bed. “Too many clothes.” This time, it was he who growled, and I heard the difference, his growl deeper, richer, sexier.

“Yes,” I agreed, yanking my shirt off of me, Byrom already stepping out of his pants by the time my shirt hit the ground.

His hands went to my button, his scent somehow more…no, not more…different, though. “Tell me you want this.” He tapped my hips, and I bucked up enough to allow him to pull the jeans from my body.

“I want you in my mouth.”

“Who says you get to go first?” He chuckled. First. He was offering…an alpha was offering to return the favor even, so to speak. And more than that, he sounded like he wanted to.

“You would—” He cut me off with his tongue swirling around my tip.

“Delicious.” He did it again and this time took me into his mouth, sucking just enough to tease and then letting me out of his mouth with another swirl of his tongue. “I’m going to make you come so hard.” He looked up at me, his eyes half-closed, the color more wolf than human. Damn, that look alone was enough to have pushed me over the edge.

"Do you like that, omega? Or would you rather I take you all the way in like this?" He took me into his mouth, swallowing as he did so, my body bucking of its own accord, my chest vibrating with a growl of desire from my wolf. He did it one, two, three more times, and each time I grew slicker and slicker. "I'll take that as a yes." His hand cupped my balls and then slid farther back. "So slick for me, omega, so very slick. I want to taste you here, too, but you are so close, aren't you?"

I nodded, unable to speak, his finger circling my entrance as his other hand pumped my cock. It was official. The man was trying to kill me.

"I'll take that as a yes as well." He entered me with the tip of his finger. "I am, too. Seeing you here, falling apart as I tease your slick hole, the taste of you on my mouth…"

He lowered his face again. "Wait," I panted, and he snapped back, his hands off of me and worry on his face. "I mean…it's not fair. I want a taste, too."

"You want me in your mouth, omega? Is that what you are saying?" He licked me from root to tip.

"Please," I pleaded.

"So needy for me. If that's what you want, why don't you come here and get it?" Like I could turn that offer down.

I had him on the bed and in my mouth in one swift and oddly graceful move. "Mmmm," I moaned around his cock, my hands curling around his ass. I licked, sucked, nibbled, and swallowed around him like it was my job, my desire to have him explode in pleasure pushing me the entire time. My cock ached for release, and try as I may, holding back was no longer an option, my climax racing into me as I cupped his balls.

Three more trips down his shaft later and he was pouring into my mouth. I greedily swallowed it down as he bellowed out my name.

I needed that.

"Same, omega." Great, I'd said it out loud. It could be worse. I could've said something embarrassing like about how I'd never come that hard in my life or something. Yeah, it could've been worse.

There was silence for a moment, I took it as an opportunity to broach the topic that had been on my mind. "Byrom?"

"Hmm?"

"Lissy explained omegas to me, and what... what they are capable of." Males having babies had thrown me for a loop, but no more than people turning into wolves, which some days I still had a hard time wrapping my head around. "How do you know I'm an omega?

Byrom smiled at me. "The same way you know I'm an alpha. Your scent. Its subtle, and since you didn't grow up in the pack, it might take time for you to notice it, but it's there. You'll sense it in others, too."

"Oh." That made sense. Since embracing my wolf I had noticed so many subtleties in scents that I could never detect before.

"Now, let's get you cleaned up." He held his hand out for me and stopped midway. "Actually, climb the rest of the way up and get comfy. I'll be back."

I did as he said, closing my eyes for just a second. A second that turned into a pitch-black room snuggled against my alpha. No, not my alpha, except maybe because of the pack hierarchy he was. Whatever. In any case, blowing the man, no matter how hot it was, probably needed to get filed away in the *Mistakes Cord Made with Men* file.

Just because I was a wolf and perpetually hard didn't mean I should randomly blow people who ignored my kiss. If he ignored that, how awkward would it be to wake up in his bed in the morning? It wasn't like he could just pretend nothing happened as we both lay there naked.

I slid out of bed carefully, not bothering to pick up my clothes, and tiptoed to my own bed, the last thought in my mind before I fell asleep focused on the omega dorms. Maybe I should ask about a room there. I didn't quite understand why they all lived together like that, but maybe it would be fun, and maybe, just maybe, I might be boner-free for a hot second, because I was already hard again and he wasn't even in the same room.

Chapter Fourteen

Byrom

I was walking on the clouds. I continued to fall deeper and deeper in…something with Cord each day. He was my complement in every way. He made me a better man and gave me a reason to smile each day, which was something I had been lacking for the past month, since losing my family.

But still, the uncertainty of the future remained. Cord tiptoed out of my room that night, and come morning, it was just like the kiss. It never happened. I tried to be okay with that. I really did, but I wanted more. But I had to tread lightly and not pressure him, so I let it go, as much as I hated it.

Cord hadn't mentioned staying forever, and he'd been asking Lissy about staying in the omega dorms. It wasn't a dorm exactly; it was just what we called the apartment-like building that some of the unmated omegas lived in until they either found their alpha or got their own home. Generally, they waited until they found their alpha.

"I'm not sure what I want to do," he'd said when I tried to ask about what his plans were. "I've been thinking about the omega dorms."

I wasn't sure, either. Cord was new to this world and still finding his paws. I was finding my way as an Alpha, still finding my own way to lead a pack. Was I ready to take on a mate and put that sort of pressure on the person I cared so much about?

My omega father had done well at the task of being the Alpha Omega. But there had been times when I'd seen him weep from the pressure. Sure, he'd always held it together for the pack. But there had been times when he hadn't been able to carry that weight silently in the comfort of his own home. My alpha father had always been there to comfort him during those times.

Would I be able to do the same?

Gods, I wished I had my parents here today. They would have loved Cord. I longed desperately for them to meet him, so much so that my heart ached with it. If only that were meant to be.

Lyle stepped into my office where I sat going through paperwork. It wasn't all full moon runs and shifting for the pack. There were financials to think about and budgets to manage.

As soon as I could, I needed to find a capable individual to take that over. The business end was becoming too much for me to handle alone. How had my father done this with all of his responsibilities?

"Didn't expect to see you in here," Lyle said.

"Then why are you in here?" I asked.

"I need the keys to the truck so I can run to town with Mia for supplies."

"Oh." I rolled my chair over to the hooks on the wall and grabbed the keys. I tossed them to Lyle.

He caught them effortlessly. "Thanks. Everything all right?"

"Yeah, just going over budget stuff." I narrowed my eyes as I lifted a receipt and stared at it for a long moment. My mind drifted to thoughts of Cord and what he was doing rather than what column to place this expense. Who was he with right now? Did he miss me? It had only been a few hours since I'd seen him, but his scent had begun to fade and was no longer fresh. I wanted to see him, hold him.

"What's wrong? We're good on money, right?"

I snapped out of my thoughts. "Yeah, of course. The financials are fine."

"So what's got you all wound up? Wait, let me guess. Cord."

Damn him for seeing right through me. I sighed. "Yeah. He's doing great. I don't really think he needs me for much at all anymore."

"And that's a problem?"

I couldn't help myself from speaking. I could only debate inside my own head for so long. I needed to talk with someone, and Lissy's advice would have been, "Just claim him, Byrom." At least I could count on Lyle to be helpful. "I don't know where we're going from this. If he doesn't need me to help him navigate pack life and being a wolf, what am I here for?"

"Dude, you're not gonna let your fated mate just go live in the omega dorms. Come on."

"Fated mate?"

Lyle's lips pursed as he stared at me. "Yeah. Fated mate."

"You think Cord is my fated?" I suspected, but wondered if it was wishful thinking on my part.

"You don't?" Lyle sat down in the chair across from me. His eyes narrowed, and his forehead crinkled. "You really don't see it?"

Hope bloomed in my chest, but I squashed it down like I had done a thousand times before. "How could I get that lucky? There hasn't been a fated mating in our generation yet," I said. Sure, I'd had the idea float through my head more than a few times, but I always squashed it down as a fairy tale.

"It's not luck, dumbass. It's fate. He's perfect for you. You're perfect for him. He balances you and the pack. He gets you to smile when you're at your grumpiest. He takes you off guard in a way I've never seen you. Even before you were named pack Alpha."

"I can't do that to him," I said. "Ask a man who wasn't born into this culture to take on that responsibility? It would crush him."

Lyle let out a low whistle. "Damn. Have some faith in

your mate, dude. Have you even tried talking to him about it? It seems like that's a choice that's up to him."

I shook my head. "There's no way. He isn't even sure what he wants to do around here. Not sure if he wants to stay."

"He won't leave you," Lyle said with a confidence that I didn't mirror. "And as far as the responsibility, he is already taking on portions of the Alpha Omega role without you realizing that. Right now, he's sitting with the young pups reading stories and playing with blocks in the courtyard while everyone else works. You should see how the little tykes have taken to him. He's a natural nurturer."

I fixed my gaze on the carpet of the office floor. With Lyle, as my brother and my Beta, I could be more vulnerable than with anyone else I knew. "I wish that I could claim him, and we could have a real mating, but I just don't know. Do you think the pack would accept him?"

"They already have."

I thought back to the night they all welcomed him into the pack. If it hadn't been for the bullshit Rance had pulled, I'd have had complete faith in what had happened there. But if one person accepted him out of duty or fear or whatever it was, couldn't there be others?

"But what about—"

The door slammed open and crashed against the wall. Both Lyle and I jerked our gaze toward the opening.

Rance stood there. Fuck it all. I had just been about to ask about Rance and his subset of followers. They wouldn't like me taking Cord on as a mate. There were still those that were wary of having Cord stay here, period. Though most of them had come around since Cord was more than carrying his weight within the pack.

"I need the truck keys," Rance barked. That was so not how that worked.

I growled. "And that's how you storm into your Alpha's presence? Slamming doors around and demanding shit?"

"Sorry, Alpha," he lied, zero sincerity hitting his words. "I assumed you were out working with the rest of the pack."

"I'm balancing the budget," I said. "If I had any trust in your math capabilities, I'd ask you to take on this job." Or anyone. But the job was too important to trust with just anyone. The pack was well off financially, but in this economy, it wouldn't take much to watch it all crumble.

"My apologies," he said, and he held up his hands in mock surrender.

"Lyle's taking the truck to town for supplies. What do you need it for?" Not that he was getting those keys.

"A trip to the lumberyard for the building project I'm working on with Laurence."

Lyle narrowed his eyes. "Didn't you just go two days ago for that?"

"We didn't get enough," Rance said.

"I thought you had to make the trip two days ago because you didn't get enough on the first trip a week ago. What the hell are you up to, Rance? Just what are you doing with these supplies?" I hadn't realized there were two trips. Lyle was great at fitting pieces like that together.

Rance's lip curled into a sneer, and Lyle stood, standing toe to toe with him.

"I don't like your tone, Lyle. If you've got an accusation, go ahead and say it out loud." Rance seethed. As if he could intimidate Lyle.

"I don't have anything yet." Lyle inched closer. "But I'm keeping an eye on you." It wasn't a threat; it was a promise.

I was as well, and Rance knew it. He hadn't yet given me the receipt from the trip two days ago, nor had I seen anything to indicate he'd even come back with new supplies. I made a mental note to look into this project he was working on. He'd been quiet since I'd called him out in front of the pack. I'd thought it was due to him falling in line, but between the bullshit at Cord's pack initiation and this, perhaps he was just waiting. The question remained: waiting for what?

"Regardless," I said, "Lyle has dibs on the truck right now. Once you give me the receipt for the previous purchase and I speak with Laurence about the project, you can take the truck to get more supplies if you need them. But Lyle will be going with you from now on."

"Whatever," he said as he stormed out of the room.

“I don’t trust that wolf,” Lyle said. “He’s up to something.”

I nodded. “I know. Follow up with Laurence and report back to me. We’ll keep an eye on him.”

Chapter Fifteen

Cord

After a weird breakfast in which we both played the amnesia game again, I thought it would be a great idea to mention the omega dorms, making the entire morning even worse. Sure, I'd mentioned them to Lissy before, but mostly out of curiosity. I didn't want to leave.

I left the house, my wolf unsettled. Was it because of the tension in the room or the way Byrom didn't try to persuade me away from the omega dorms or the post-blowjob amnesia we both seemed to share? I didn't know. I had a feeling it was a combination of all three.

And I didn't like it.

I headed down the path to the school. The pups would be at recess still, and it would give me time to get my new book ready. I loved reading to the pups, and they ate it up. Mia told me it gave her time to do whatever it was that teachers did at their desks.

"Cord," Casper called out. I swore he'd grown three inches since his first shift.

"Casper, ready for story time?" I asked as I reached up

and caught the ball he tossed my way.

“Yeah. Miss Mia said that you were reading us one about witches.” Other children ran up and joined us as we spoke. “I hope they are the bad kind, not the kind with glitter and stuff.”

“Oh, don’t you worry. These witches turn children into,” I lowered my voice, “mice.”

And that had the entire class lined up five minutes ahead of schedule, all of them needing to hear about the evil witches.

I had a blast with the kids, loving the way they were so enveloped in the story, and when it was time to leave, none of us were ready to give up the book. “I’ll be back,” I promised as I closed the book. “But you guys have hunting today, and you don’t want to miss that.”

Mia instructed them to grab a snack and head outside to meet the Betas that were going to instruct them today.

“Do they ever catch anything?” I asked Mia as the last one walked out.

“No. Which is why I have them eat first. Mostly they are still in the watching phase, although Finn caught a mouse the other day.”

“Isn’t he too young to shift?” He was one of the youngest in the group, Casper and the recent new shifts having at least a few years on him.

“He built a trap. Said hunting took too much energy.” She laughed. “The kid is too smart for his own good.”

"I guess I'll be on my way." I set the book down on her desk. "Same time next time?"

"Sounds good. Are you off somewhere in particular?" she asked, sticking her pencil in her bun. For someone young and hot, she sure had some old lady habits.

"Not really. Need some help with something?" I'd gladly spend the day at the school. I didn't have the patience or knowhow to be a teacher, but I could play, read, and correct spelling tests like a boss.

"Nothing like that. I was just thinking how the Betas are here and how Byrom is so bad at eating while he is working." She walked around to the window, and I could see her lips counting. How many times a day did she count the class? Probably a bazillion. They were not the best at staying put. "It might be nice for him to have some lunch company."

"You aren't very subtle," I teased as I headed to the door.

"I never said I was. Have fun at lunch." She gave a half wave and wandered back to her desk.

I stepped outside, watched the pups for a minute, and thought about what Mia said, quickly making the decision. I was taking Byrom on a lunch date.

***

"Knock knock." I stood at the threshold of Byrom's office door. "Can I come in?"

"Always." He put his pencil down and looked up at me with that smile, the one that said I was special, even if his words never did.

“I was hoping to borrow the truck keys.” And just like that, his smile dropped. I thought I’d been so clever in my date asking, and I already made him sad. “Never mind,” I mumbled. Why was I so shitty at this?

“Lyle has them.” There was more to that story, but I didn’t push. “What did you need it for? I can call him back.”

“I—this is going to sound stupid—I was going to take you to town for lunch.”

“Like a date?” And just like that, his smile was back.

“Yeah. Too human?”

“Just human enough. We can take a car.” He rolled his chair over to a pegboard filled with keys and snatched a keyring. “What kind of food were you thinking?”

“I hadn’t gotten that far yet.” I’d been so nervous he’d say no, I never went past the ask-him stage. “Do you like nachos?”

“With olives?” He scrunched up his nose.

“I’ll eat all the big bad olives. I promise.”

“Then I love nachos.” He shut the book he was working on and put it in his desk. “Who’s driving?”

“Who is Byrom, for three hundred dollars?” I held out my hand for him, and he took it. “The diner is supposed to have the best nachos in town, as weird as that sounds.

Willing to risk it?"

"With you? Always." *Do not read too much into this. Do not read too much into this.* I was so reading too much into this.

Byrom drove us to town, where we ate in a packed diner and talked about my time at school, what it was like being a twin, and random things one would talk about on a first date. This wasn't the way of shifters, and I got that. I did. Their version of dating would be shifting together and going for a hunt, rather than ordering a meal at a diner. But I grew up human, and the human side of me needed this, too. And Byrom seemed on board with it. I was more than a random blowjob to him, even if he pretended it never happened. How much more? I didn't know. But more was enough. At least for now.

The nachos were meh, the company magnificent, and the lunch date absolutely perfect with the exception of no good-bye kiss. Although, to be fair, when it was time to say good-bye, the Betas were all returning to the office about I didn't even know what, and a kiss would have been inappropriate at best.

How I longed for another kiss.

"Swing by after practice?" he asked as I gave a half wave good-bye.

"As long as I can still walk." I was only half teasing. Today, the goal was for me to shift midair, and I saw a lot of hard landings in my future.

"You'll be great." He gave my hand a squeeze as he

mumbled something under his breath. It was probably best I didn't know what. "Go kick ass, little wolf."

And kick ass I did—after falling on my ass seven consecutive times.

Chapter Sixteen

Byrom

Three hours after our lunch date, the click of the front door had my attention snapping up from the paperwork in front of me. My senses heightened; my nose twitched as the air around me shifted. All this because someone had walked into my home. Nobody had even walked into the room yet.

Immediately, I knew it was Cord who had returned home. My wolf recognized his presence three rooms apart.

I stood up. My feet hurried across the room as if I couldn't bear to be apart from Cord one moment longer. The closer I got to my mate, the faster my heart raced. Lunch hadn't been enough. I wasn't sure any amount of together time would be.

Not your mate. Not yet, I scolded myself. Cord was human. Today's date only amplified that fact. He needed wooing, not *mate me and you will have my heart until my dying breath*. The way humans married and divorced, he'd never believe the words even if I was selfish enough to say them.

"Cord?"

"Yeah?" he called from the kitchen. "I was just putting this away." He held up a Tupperware container. "Lissy sent over dinner for us for later. I was going to come get you."

"I couldn't wait." It was the truth.

"Are you hungry?" he offered.

I shook my head, though I had been working hard and the nachos didn't quite cut it for a filling lunch. Not with my metabolism.

Just then, my traitorous stomach rumbled.

Cord smiled. "I'll go ahead and warm it up. You're probably hungry after having basically a snack for lunch."

I smiled. His words mimicked my thoughts as if we were already on the same wavelength.

Mates.

"We should talk about last night," I said before I could think better of it. It had been the third entity at lunch, just sitting there waiting for us to invite it into our conversation. In the car, it felt too impersonal, neither of us being able to look at each other, and then at the restaurant, there were too many ears around us. There were no excuses here, in my—our—the kitchen.

He shook his head. "No. I just—I'm so embarrassed." Not the answer I expected, but then again, he had all day to wonder why I never said anything. He didn't, either, but I had a feeling that was where his humanness came in.

“You shouldn’t be,” I said. “Wolves are run by their instincts.”

“I get that,” he said. “But I’m not used to it, and I’m not used to just random blowjobs.”

I ran a hand through my hair. “Well, neither am I. That’s not what I was saying. Has anyone talked to you about what it means to have a mate?”

Cord’s gaze snapped up from the microwave he had begun to program with the time for my food.

“Yeah, I mean, I’ve heard some of the other omegas talk about their mates or finding their mates. What’s that got to do with last night?”

“Well, it’s just that.” I stepped closer to him. I lifted a hand as if to touch him. I opened my mouth to speak, but nothing came out. “Ugh, see, um. You and I—well, it seems that—I think that you and I are mates.”

Cord’s jaw dropped. “What? What does that even mean?”

I ran a hand through my hair. “Well—”

“How would we know?”

Shit. I hadn’t been prepared for all the questions. Young wolves learned this stuff from their parents, and I wasn’t prepared to have the *talk*. “Sex,” I said. “Usually, the pack Alpha picks their mate when they’re named Alpha or before. They don’t rule alone. But I became Alpha so suddenly…”

"You didn't get a chance to pick a mate."

I shook my head. "And he wouldn't have been my fated mate anyway. We can pick our mates, or fate can provide them for us. Some wolves wait to find their fated. Others choose to pick their mates."

"And now you think it's a good time to have one, cause you think I'm your fated, or are you picking me?" Cord's eyes were wide with curiosity.

Was that good or bad? I wasn't sure.

"No, that's not it at all." Damn, I was mucking this up. "This is different. Um, sometimes Alphas don't wait for their fated. They just pick who would be a good Alpha Omega for the pack. I was never comfortable with that idea. I wanted to wait for my fated."

"Is being the Alpha and not having a mate bad?" Cord asked.

"Not exactly. But having an Alpha Omega at my side would provide balance. Some pack members think that I should have one or I should step down as Alpha."

"Who?" Cord bristled. "Rance? He can go fuck himself. He isn't mated, either, and he isn't half that alpha that you are."

I grinned. My omega, my defender. "Yes, Rance has an issue with it. But it's just an excuse for him to question my leadership. But that isn't why I am talking to you about it. I—"

Cord held up a hand and stopped me from speaking. "I'm

not even sure what I'm doing right now, Byrom. I love the people here, love spending time with everyone, but this is a lot to take in. This idea of a mate, it seems…" He bit his lip.

"Crazy, right?"

"Crazy, and also right—completely and totally right. I feel like I could easily get lost with you. But I've never relied on another person. Ever. And that terrifies me. I just don't know if it's a good idea for us to get involved any further."

My heart ached for him. I stepped forward, grabbed his hand, and held it to my chest, breathing in his sweet cherry blossom scent that had intrigued me from the very first day. "I would never ever leave you or hurt you in any possible way. You would be the most cherished mate in any pack, ever. That I can promise you."

Cord's gaze searched my face. "I believe you. But I think I might need time to process all this. Seems like each day something new gets thrown at me. Just the other day, I was a regular human, now I'm a wolf, part of a pack, an omega, and I could be the Alpha Omega? It's a lot, Byrom."

I nodded. "I know it is, little wolf. I'm here for you if you need anything." Always. Even if that thing he needed was to be away from me.

Chapter Seventeen

Cord

“Byrom?” I pulled open the microwave to take out our dinner, some kind of casserole that smelled delicious.

“Cord.”

“So this fated mate thing…is that why… Never mind. Let’s eat.” I popped the lid and set the piping hot container on the counter.

“Is that why what?” He came up behind me, reaching over my head for the plates. “You can ask me anything…always.” He kissed the side of my head and placed the two plates on the counter. That was new. It wasn’t the heady need of our first kiss or even the over-the-top lust-induced frenzy that was our blowjob hook-up. It was affectionate and, dare I say, sweet.

“Is that why I’m always so…you know?” I opened my eyes wide, trying to do that thing they do in movies to indicated sex and probably just looked like I had an eyelash in my eye or something.

“Randy? Why you are so randy?” And he did the same thing I did, only instead of being an awkward mess, he was sexy as fuck.

“Randy?” I shook my head in mirth. “Really? People don’t still say that word, you know.” Or maybe they did. I peopled minimally before this whole pack thing, and at the time, it was fine. Now? Now I craved the togetherness. It was weird. Awesome, but for sure weird.

“But is it accurate?” He pulled me flush to his body, our cocks pressed together. Yep, accurate.

“I guess.” Knew. Same difference. “I mean, I was going to talk about being hard all the stupid time, not that that sounds better.”

I buried my face in his chest, my cheeks burning. This shouldn’t be embarrassing, and yet…there I was blushing like an innocent, and while this whole possible-relationship-slash-fated-mates thing was new to me, I’d had some hot nights in my past. Sex itself was far from new to me.

“Don’t cover your face, omega mine. There is nothing to be ashamed of. It isn’t like you are the only one here in the same predicament.”

“Predicament?” I looked up at him, trying to figure out if he was being silly or all thesaurus boy when it came to important conversations, and yeah, this conversation felt important. Almost too important.

“It made you smile.” There was that. “And how have you not noticed how many showers I take?” Was he saying…whoa…no way.

“I figured you ran in the woods a lot.” And now an

entirely different vision was dancing around in my head, a better one. Sexier, at least.

"I do, but that wasn't why. I was searching for relief." Yeah, now he was just saying words to get me to smile. Two could play that game.

"Cold showers aren't relief," I quipped.

"I need to spell it out, I see." He brought his lips close to my ear, his breath tickling my neck. "I was thinking of you as I made myself come."

"So you are perpetually hard as a rock even after you—you know—shower."

"Pretty much." He nipped my ear. "Yeah."

"What do you think about when you…shower…specifically?" Because damn if I didn't want to join him in said shower.

"My omega likes dirty talk." He raked me with his eyes.

"Is that okay?" I ran a finger across his chest, feeling emboldened. His eyes were so feral, and his scent was even richer than the night before. He liked where this was going. Fuck. I did, too.

"That's hot as fuck." He took my hand in his. "Come with me. Let's get you naked and on my bed."

"Why? I mean, I'm going to because…well, we already established why, but…" Please let it be to do all the dirty things my mind was throwing at me.

"Trust me." The thing was I did trust him and not just to bring me to his bed. There was something about him that had me trusting him completely. Was that the fated mates thing? I didn't even know, but it was nice. So very nice.

He led me through the house and up the stairs to his bedroom, stopping us in the doorway, his body pressed against mine.

"You asked what I think about in the shower…" I nodded. "This is what I think about: you on my bed naked and waiting for me, playing with your hard cock." I took that as a hint and ran over to the bed, shucking my clothes as I did and only stumbling once—fine, twice, but I recovered gracefully from the second one. I sat on the bed, my back against the headboard, my left knee up so he could get a glimpse of my entrance as I slowly pumped my cock with my right hand. He stood in the doorway, his jeans visibly tight, his eyes focused on my hand and its leisurely trip up and down my erection.

"Like this?"

He swallowed deeply.

"That part is always the same." He stalked over like I was his prey. Gods, I loved being his prey. "Other parts vary." He winked and then pulled his shirt up and over his head.

"Like a 'choose your own adventure'?" I sassed, still playing with myself as his hand went to his button.

"Sort of." He pulled down his zipper and dropped his jeans, his cock bouncing up and down at its freedom. No underwear to be seen.

“The alpha comes in and sees his omega on the bed, naked, his cock in his hand.” I used my best sex phone operator voice. “Does he: A. join him on the bed and join in on the fun, or B. tell him he’s a naughty omega and needs a spanking?”

“You are going to kill me, little wolf.” He stepped out of his jeans.

“A or B?”

I could practically see him playing out the two options in his head.

“A,” he finally decided as he crawled on the bed to me. “Maybe B later.”

“That’s not how this works, alpha,” I lied. It totally was how this worked. I liked this game almost too much. I loosened my grip, not wanting things to be over before they started.

“The alpha joins his omega on the bed and wraps his fingers around the omega’s cock,” he batted my hand away playfully and did just that, “jerking it a couple of times as the omega watches the precum forming on his alpha’s tip and licks his lips.” I added a little bite to my lip as he watched my lips like they held the secret to all good things. “The omega is so slick for his alpha.” Not a lie. It was beginning to drip down my crack. “Should the alpha: A. kiss his omega and continue with what he is currently doing, or B. play with his omega’s needy hole?”

“Kiss and play with all of him,” Byrom countered and took my lips with his, exploring my body with his hands as he owned my mouth, his fingers eventually circling my hole as I bucked into his hand, wanting—needing more. Needing him inside—fingers—cock—tongue. I wasn't picky. He ended our kiss, and I whimpered.

He chuckled.

Of course he did.

"Now that the omega is breathless and begging," Byrom took over my story, which was good because my brain was no longer braining, "should the alpha: A. slide inside his omega's aching entrance and slowly bring him to climax?" Yes, that. "Or B. flip him over on his hands and knees and go hard and fast until he fills him with his cock until they both collapse on the bed in a sweaty pile of limbs." Or that.

"That."

"That?" he asked. He had no right to be that sexy

"B," I barked out. He gave me a knowing look. "You are so much better at this game than I am. B."

One single cocky nod. "B."

I got on my hands and knees. "Now?"

"Look at you all sexy and waiting. I can't wait to slide into you—the alpha said, meaning every word." Oh, we were still on that. Fuck yeah. "And then he lined himself up with his wiggly omega, grabbing his hip with one hand and holding on tight, loving the way his omega was squirming with need. He fed his cock into him slowly, watching his cock disappear into his hole and feeling like he was coming home." He pushed himself in me slowly…so freaking slowly, it was torture, exquisite torture. I pushed back into him, his hand on my hip stopping me from reaching my goal. "The omega had no patience."

"The omega picked B. Hard and fast. Hard. And. Fast."

"He did pick B." His other hand found my hip, and he pushed the rest of the way in in one smooth motion. "Let me know when—"

"Now. Move now." And he did. In and out, hard and fast just like I begged, demanded, asked, I didn't even know what anymore. Heck, I didn't know my name. All I could do was feel as he pumped in and out of me, filling me so completely and hitting the perfect spot with each thrust.

"I'm…I can't…I'm going to…"

"And the omega: A. wanted his alpha to touch his cock and make him come, or B. wanted his alpha to slow down and keep him on edge."

"A. A. A. A," I begged, and he reached down, barely touching me as I exploded, shooting cum all over the bed. "Fuck me, alpha," I cried out, and he increased his speed, his warm cum shooting inside me as his cock swelled.

My gums ached, my heart pounded, and my wolf pushed to the forefront. *Ours. Claim. Ours. Claim.*

Byrom's arms came around me, his front to my back, and he rolled us on our sides.

We were locked together in a way that had never

happened to me before.

"Wow. Um, Byrom, is this a wolf thing?" I couldn't complain. It was amazing. His cock still buried in me, locked by something, whatever it was, it didn't seem to be going away.

He nuzzled into my neck. "This is a fated thing, omega."

"What?"

"I'm sorry. I should have explained better before, well… now. It's a knot. It only ever happens with your fated mate. That's how you know your fated."

"But you suspected that I was…"

He kissed my neck and I moaned against him. Each touch felt like a jolt of electricity through every nerve ending. "Yes, I suspected you were my fated. Now we know." And he sounded pleased at the idea. Smug even.

"Wow." Tears sprang to my eyes. Fate finally brought me to the place where I belonged and in the arms of an Alpha. At least knotted like this, I didn't need to look at him as I processed my emotions. "I've never really been much of a cuddler."

"Do you mind?" He kissed my shoulder again and held me tighter, like he didn't want to let go, but I knew he would if I asked.

"You're different." I reached behind me to cup his cheek.

"Because I'm your fated?"

"No," I insisted, though my wolf told me I was wrong. My heart, too. "Because you're Byrom. You have all this responsibility on your shoulders, and you saw me alone and scared and unsure, and you saved me. You didn't have to, but you did." Had Rance been Alpha, I would've been dead. Period.

"It was the right thing to do."

"But was it within the rules?"

"Well…"

"Exactly." I leaned my head back, trying to somehow be closer to him than I already was, which was crazy. We were joined by his knot. There was nothing closer than that. "You're different in all the best of ways."

"My Alpha Omega deserves the best." Alpha Omega—his beginning and end—the pack's beginning and end. *Not now. Don't think about that now.* It was too much, the entire thing just too much. I pushed all thoughts of that down. It wasn't even like I had agreed to anything but sex yet. That could wait.

I opened and closed my mouth a few times, my jaw still throbbing.

"Are you okay?" he asked. "I can feel you doing something."

"I was just moving my jaw. It hurts."

"Did it start when you came?"

"Yeah. How did you know?"

"Mine hurts, too. Our wolves want to claim each other. It's what mates do. They mark each other so all other wolves know they are claimed." And he sounded four bazillion times more confident and happier about that than I did. If only I could have half his confidence in this fated mates thing. Instead, I had a growing case of imposter syndrome. There was no way, me—a foster kid all grown up who never had a family and who didn't even know he was a wolf—could be good enough for the pack Alpha.

No. Way.

And that sucked.

Big. Time.

"Stay with me, Cord, please?"

I hesitated. I wanted to. I knew he was asking for forever and not just for tonight. He wanted me to be the Alpha Omega officially, but I held back. "I'm—I'm not sure, Byrom. I need time."

He kissed my neck, ever the patient alpha. "Then you shall have it."

Chapter Eighteen

Byrom

Things had been perfect. I thought for a moment that I had begun to hit my stride as an Alpha. I'd found my omega, and he was amazing in every single way. The pack was happy and content, comforted by the fact that their future Alpha Omega was close by, even if they didn't realize that was what brought them the comfort. Morale was up, and our pack was moving forward with our healing from having lost our previous Alpha.

Once we had the mating ceremony and Cord was presented as the official Alpha Omega, then things would really fall into place.

I just needed to convince him.

Instead, I'd scared Cord away by asking him to stay. I'd dropped the weight of that responsibility into his lap without thinking about it.

It was so easy for me to forget that he had gone his entire life without understanding pack dynamics. But this was a lot to throw on him at once. We hadn't spoken much since I'd asked him to stay with me permanently. I promised him time, and he would get it. But my wolf didn't like it. I didn't like it, either, but it was necessary.

Cord scurried around the house cleaning, cooking, putting together little meals for each and every person in the pack, it seemed. He baked a batch of cookies for Mia and her pups and a loaf of banana bread for Taylor because they had mentioned that they liked it. He listened to their problems when they needed an ear, and he always made everyone feel welcome, even Rance, who was far from welcome.

I hated that I was going to have to deal with him soon instead of just brushing it aside and hoping he got his act together. But I hated the idea of what would come of any challenge that took place. Blood would be spilled, and it wouldn't be mine. I just wasn't ready for that yet.

Cord was doing everything that came naturally to an Alpha Omega; even if he couldn't quite see it himself, I saw it. And it made me hungry for what could be. I saw now why tradition had Alphas mated before they took their position. He balanced me out—made me a better Alpha.

It was late into the evening, and I could no longer sit still and ignore the elephant in the room. My wolf paced within me, anxious for us to go and claim our mate, let our entire pack know that he was ours. But my human side, the smarter side, knew we needed to wait for him to be ready.

"Cord?" I said as I stepped into the kitchen.

Cord stood at the sink, elbow-deep in dishwater. He jumped when I spoke.

“I’m going to bed.” I didn’t need to let him know. I never had before. But I used it as an excuse to speak to him.

“All right. Okay. Good night.”

“Dinner was delicious,” I said.

“Thank you.” He smiled, not quite meeting my eyes.

“You’re welcome.”

It was on the tip of my tongue to bring up our discussion from the other day, ask him what I could do to help to smooth the way over. But I knew he just needed time, and pushing him to make a decision would never help. I didn’t want to force him. I wanted him to come to me because he wanted to. I wanted Cord to want to be here, to want to be with me.

“Good night,” I said with a smile.

Cord turned back to his task.

I crept up the stairs and crawled into my bed. My sheets had smelled like him ever since the other night, though they had been freshly cleaned. Laundry was another thing that Cord had begun doing for me and other members of the pack who were unable. He was constantly finding ways to be helpful, and the pack was grateful for it.

I rolled around restlessly. The darkness of the night called to my wolf to shift and run. But I had an early morning meeting. And besides, I didn’t want the forest. What I really wanted was downstairs.

It seemed like hours later, I was still staring at the ceiling.

Sleep came to me in short jaunts. Never restful. My dreams were filled with Cord and nothing else.

The door creaked as it opened, and I sat upright. My vision adjusted to the darkness easily. I didn't sense danger. Instead, I recognized the scent of my omega as it filled the room.

Cord stood in the doorway. He shifted his weight from one foot to the other.

I pulled the covers back, inviting him next to me. He climbed in.

"I feel like I haven't slept in days," he said. "It's like I can't rest unless I am at your side."

"I know. I feel the same. Stay here with me tonight," I said.

"I don't want to sleep," he replied as he slid in behind me. "And my head…it's racing a thousand miles a minute."

Not what I thought he had in mind when he said he couldn't sleep, but if being by my side and unloading the stress of his days to me made him happier, I was there for it.

"You don't have to do so much. Around the pack, I mean." I brushed a stray hair from his brow. "There is no expectation that you do so."

"I need to feel like I'm contributing. But that's the thing. I went to school and earned my degree, and since I graduated, I've had shit jobs or now no job, and never once used my degree." My stomach dropped. I had no idea he was feeling this way. I had assumed that his picking up bits and pieces were out of desire to do them, not out of a feeling of obligation. Fuck that. He needed to do what felt right for him, and if that meant not being the perfect textbook version of an Alpha Omega, then so be it. We weren't in the times of old, and I refused to treat my omega like we were.

"You want a job?" I'd drive him every day if he did.

"No. Not really. I mean, yes, but also, I have skills, and they're not just doing the things I've been doing. I have a business degree with a minor in accounting, and I feel like I can be doing more to help, and instead I'm cooking and cleaning and—they are all good important things, you know, but also…I'm being ungrateful. You gave me a place to stay and covered my debts, and here I am all whiny because I—I'm sorry." He snuggled into me as he let it all out. He didn't hold back.

"Omega mine, never feel you can't tell me what you're feeling. Never."

"It's just you've done so much for me," he whispered against my chest.

"You're my omega, even if you never choose me to be your alpha. And if you want to use your degree, we will make it happen." I already had half an idea forming. I loathed doing the pack accounting. I also didn't want to force my Betas to do it. They were already overworked. I could trust Cord. I needed to talk to my brother before offering it to him, but my wolf was already simmering down just knowing I was working on a plan to make our omega at peace.

"You would do that for me? You would help me get a job when the pack would want my job to be just an Alpha Omega? Not just. That came out wrong."

"I think we already covered this. I would do anything for you, and the pack will love you as you are when—if you pick us. Now how about we get some sleep and we can revisit this tomorrow?" I kissed the top of his head.

"I can't sleep like this." He moved his hips just enough to have his rock-hard cock pressed against my thigh.

"I wonder what we can do about that…hmmm." I reached down and traced it with my finger, continuing down until I reached his slick hole. "Are you needy here, too?" He was, so slick and ready. My wolf was pushing to the forefront, begging for me to take him, mark him, mate him.

He was going to have to wait. Tonight wasn't about that. Tonight was about making my omega feel as special as he was, making him feel the emotions I felt for him deep down and not just the lust that was always at the surface, giving him the comfort that came with knowing I loved him just the way he was, even if it wasn't time for the words yet.

"You know I am." He rolled off his side and onto his back, spreading his legs a little wider and tugging my arm just enough to let me know where he wanted me to be.

"I can take care of that." I settled between his legs and kissed him soundly. "I can't wait to be inside you." I nipped his ear.

"Should we use protection? Since I can get pregnant and all that."

I pushed myself up on my arms so I could look him in the eyes when I answered him. Thank goodness for shifter vision.

"Whatever you want…but know this: if you were to carry my baby, it would make me the happiest alpha in the world." He gasped. "And no, I will not pressure you to do so, but know it is so."

"Really?" Astonishment filled his voice. I needed to always remember how little he knew about our kind and what it meant to be fated mates. He needed to be reminded of the things others grew up knowing. He needed to both know and believe he was my one and only, for always and forever.

"Okay." He pulled me close to him. "Make love to me, alpha."

"I would be honored."

"And you can knot me…I mean, if you want to."

"Oh, I want to." I nipped at his bottom lip the way he liked. "Thank you, omega mine. Thank you for trusting me tonight, for being everything I could've hoped for in a mate, and for being you."

He answered me with a kiss.

Chapter Nineteen

Cord

"I think it's time I get the rest of my things." It had been the weird thing unspoken between all of this. Technically, I still had my apartment; the leasing office had agreed to being paid because they liked money, but also wanted the rest of the term paid for. And I got that. It was their business.

It also sucked because I was bringing in zero money, and my cooking wasn't awful, but it sure wasn't worth the amount of money that was spent to get me out of the hole I'd dug myself into.

"We can do that." He picked up his glass of OJ and drank it down. "Is that why you aren't eating today?" He pointed to my plate.

"Maybe. I guess." I hadn't really thought about it, but I wasn't very hungry, either.

"How about we get your things and have an early lunch in town?" he offered, picking up his plate and glass as he rose. "Maybe we could go to that sports bar near your old apartment and get burgers."

“I started work there and then…things happened.”

“You mean, you shifted into your wolf the first time and missed your next shift?” he said as he set his plate in the sink. “Is that the job you want? I could maybe help get it back.” He was too sweet, even if misguided.

“Sure. You can just tell them I turned into a wolf and you were supposed to kill me but instead decided to save me, and now that I’m not gonna be killed, you thought maybe they should give me a second chance. Something like that?”

He picked up my plate. “I was thinking something more along the lines of, ‘Whoa, look at that sexy omega. I’d buy all the drinks from him.’ Or the equivalent.” Byrom winked at me. “They’d hire you back immediately.”

“Yeah, that’ll work.” I shook my head and rolled my eyes. “But I appreciate the offer. What do you think about my stuff?” If I was going to be here full-time, it was best to just do it all Band-Aid style.

“I’ll grab the truck keys, and we can go now, and we can find a new place for lunch.”

“I never agreed to lunch.”

“Omega, if your alpha wants to woo you, let him woo you.”

“Well, if wooing is the plan, I best put on a nicer shirt.” Or at least one without a hole.

***

Driving back into town was an odd sensation. It had been my home and yet not, and coming back had me on edge, which made no sense, but so be it.

"That looks like a wooing place." Byrom indicated a small Italian place on our left.

"I guess. I mean, if you like real tablecloths and all that." I had no idea if that was even true, having never set foot in the place, but it screamed expensive. "Cal's has good burgers."

"I can do something better than burgers for my omega."

"First of all, there is nothing better than an olive burger. Full stop. And even if such a thing existed, which it does not, they have the world's best apple pie. The sign even says so." I'd only been in a couple of times when I first moved into town, but just the thought of their juicy burger and onion rings had my mouth watering and my stomach growling.

"Cal's it is." He pulled into my old complex. "We can keep or get rid of anything you want to in here." He gave my knee a squeeze.

"I want some of it." I already had a mental list. "But it isn't nice enough for your place."

"Our place," he growled. Guess that was a conversation for a different time. "And we can make it work. If you love it…it stays."

"I wouldn't say I loved any of it, but some of it means something to me, so thanks." We got out of the truck, and I froze. It hadn't been long ago that I came home here every day, and it was fine, or at least fine enough. Now that I'd lived in a real home—which shouldn't have been a first for someone of my age, but it was—and the more I looked at my apartment door, the more I understood how true it was.

"Let's go." He took my hand, and I found the strength to continue the short distance to the door.

I fumbled with my keys and pushed it open, the stale smell from it being closed hitting me like a brick wall.

"The small table beside my bed, the one with the old computer on it, I built that myself." From scraps I found at the dump, but still. I made it. "The computer is really not much good for anything. It is an old OS that is no longer supported and really is only good for typing and printing, but sometimes I needed that. We can probably recycle it at the collection station in town. We might even get a few bucks for it." I doubted it, but they claimed to pay, so why not try?

"We can do that." He walked past me to where my computer lived and started to disconnect it.

"I'm just going to collect my mail," I called to him. "I'll be right back." I walked to the communal area and opened my box, grabbing all of the mail, even the junk, and brought it back to my place, needing to be near Byrom; my wolf was very unsettled.

"I'm back," I called into the apartment as I stepped inside. He was fast. The table was already gone.

"That table is impressive. I know you went to school for

business, but have you thought about possibly using it to start your own, making furniture from reclaimed items?" He was dead serious.

"I'm no expert. I just made it with what I found, and it turned out okay."

"And the piece over there?" He pointed to my chair. "And there?" A small cabinet that had once held pantry items. "You made those, too, right?"

"Yeah."

"Then you have skill. It might not be what you want to do in life, and that's okay, but you have a gift to see what will work together and the ability to piece them together." His pride in my work meant more than he could possibly know.

"Thanks. I'll consider it." And I would. I did love making the items. At the time, it felt so grown up, and it also meant I had some furniture.

"You didn't make any of the rest, did you?"

"Nope. We can chuck it all."

"Anything good?" he asked, glancing at the pile of mail.

"I don't know. Let me check." Junk. Junk. More junk. My electric bill. Junk. And an envelope from my boss. "Looks like I just got a paycheck or something. The rest is all junk."

"No bills?"

“The electric, but it should be close to nothing since no one was here.” I tore open the envelope, and sure enough, it was a check, but with the check came a letter. I read it. Once. Twice. Three times.

“Omega. Tell me what’s wrong.” His arms were around me, and I couldn’t form the words, instead handing him the letter that said I was no longer a contractor with them, which I had seen coming, but that I was no longer eligible to do contract work at any of their offices and affiliated companies, followed by a huge list of places. I was blackballed.

“This isn’t legal.” He squeezed me closer. “It isn’t. They are just being asses. We can fight it. You didn’t miss a lot of time, and we can have the pack healer write you a note—she’s a nurse, too. We can fix this.”

“I don’t need you fixing my messes.” I stepped out of his arms, refusing to cry. “The kitchen stuff can all go. Maybe we can donate it to the local free store and help someone starting out.”

Because changing the conversation was the only way of keeping me from breaking down, proving to myself once again, I wasn’t strong enough to be the pack’s Alpha Omega.

But what choice did I have? It was all or nothing, and I was too weak to let go of Byrom. He had already become my everything.

Chapter Twenty

Byrom

My wolf howled and paced, sensing the distress of its mate, right next to us, but we could do nothing.

Cord hadn't said much since reading the letter that essentially terminated his employment and blackballed him from other agencies. He didn't even offer more than one-word answers as we ate at Cal's, eating the burger he swore was the best food ever. Although eat was far from the best word choice. He nibbled at best and turned down pie. He was hurting so much, and I just wanted to fix it all. If only I knew how.

I understood his job was important to him, even if it wasn't what he longed for as a career, and could see it hurt him deeply. Growing up in the pack, I didn't understand why a job like this one held such importance to him. He had a different job now. Being with the pack. And being with me. Caring for us, contributing to the pack.

Why couldn't he see that? How could I help him to see that?

"I'd like you to come back to the packhouse with me."

Cord shook his head, not looking at me, instead just staring out the window. "I want to stay in the dorm. It's better for me there."

A growl snuck out of my chest before I could stop it. And he looked at me sharply.

"You're not the alpha over me, Byrom. I can make my own choices."

"I know. I'm not trying to tell you what to do." I wanted to be the Alpha with him, with him at my side. We were equals; couldn't he see that? I was nothing without him.

"The pack is never going to accept me as the Alpha Omega. I'm not sure I accept the idea. I can't." He shook his head, tears pooling in the corner of his eyes. "I'm not one of you, Byrom."

My hands gripped the steering wheel. We turned onto the lane that led us back to the packhouse, and my wolf settled, knowing that we were closer to home and our mate was at least safe back in our territory, no longer in the city, where he could leave and leave us behind.

"You are one of us, Cord. You are a wolf."

He let out a whimper, his wolf sneaking to the surface. "I know that. And I feel it. I'm more at home with the pack than I've ever been before."

"Then stay with me."

"No," he said. "I can't. There's too much going on in my head right now. I don't know what's right, wrong, or what my future is."

"I'm your future. The pack is your future." Panic rose in my chest, all thoughts of letting Cord come to his own decisions thrown out the window. My wolf sensed that our omega was going to leave, and he wanted nothing of the sort.

Mate. Take. Claim.

"I need time, Byrom. Can't you please see that?"

This time, I stopped the growl. But my wolf didn't like it. I would need to shift soon and run, just to stop myself from doing something stupid.

"I don't know if I can handle you staying in the dorm. My wolf hates the idea of you being away from us."

"I know, I can feel it. My wolf doesn't like it, either."

"Then why leave? Trust your wolf."

Cord hung his head and wrung his hands in his lap. His voice was small and far away. "I'm not like you, Byrom. I haven't known about being a wolf and pack life forever. This is still new to me. You need to give me space."

"I don't want to," I admitted. "I don't know if I can handle being away from you."

"You can and you will. You don't have a choice. Maybe things will be different in the morning or in a couple of days, but right now, I just need space."

I swallowed thickly, biting back my desire to throw him over my shoulder and keep him in my home, with me. But that was barbaric and not what he needed right now. I needed to be strong and give him the things he asked for, even if it hurt to do so. "All right. I will do that. But can I please see you tomorrow?"

Cord nodded. "I think so."

I pulled the truck to a stop outside the house and pushed open the door. Fur erupted on my arms, and my canines dropped as I barely kept my wolf in check.

"I'll have Lyle and the other Betas keep watch over you."

Cord had gotten out of the truck and stared at me from over the hood. He held up a hand. "No, Byrom. No special treatment. I'm just like any of the other omegas that stay in that dorm." Cord stepped onto the porch. "I'm going to go grab my stuff. Are you okay?"

I turned away from him. I couldn't answer. "I'm going for a run." My wolf cried out as he went in the opposite direction of our mate. I lost control and shifted into my wolf form and took off into the forest.

Chapter Twenty-One

Cord

I packed a small bag and headed off to the omega dorms, wishing I could take it all back but knowing this was for the best.

My wolf didn't agree, begging me to run, to catch our mate and make him ours for real. I couldn't do that. I wasn't strong enough to be his mate. I wasn't strong enough to be anyone's mate. I couldn't even lose a job I hated without falling apart.

I slung my bag over my shoulder and went on the search for Lyle. I knew the omega dorm was open for me, but other than that, the logistics were beyond me. Lyle would help me, even though it would hurt to see him, his face too similar to Byrom's.

I wandered around the pack lands, eventually finding Lyle helping an older omega with a broken tree limb.

"What's up?" He set down his saw and walked over to me. "My brother treating you well?" He had a lilt in his tone, like he'd been teasing, and you could see the second he realized all was not right in my world. "Shit. Sorry. What's wrong? Need me to call Byrom?"

“No!” I said far too forcefully. “I mean, you don’t need to call him. I came to you for something else.”

“You need me to kick his ass? Cause I will. No alpha should hurt their omega…ever.” He was serious, too. Holy shit. He would fight his brother for me…me, a wolf who didn’t know how to be a wolf and who just randomly showed up.

“It’s not his fault. It’s mine.” I sighed. “Can you help me settle into the omega dorms? Like, is there paperwork or something I need to do?”

“There’s nothing you could do to have him not want you.” He held up one finger, turned his head, and called out, “I’ll be back in a bit, Hank.” He held out his hand for my bag, and my stubborn ass held it tighter. He just shook his head. “I’ll take you because you asked and that is my job. I’d rather take you home where you belong.”

Except I didn’t belong there.

Why did he have to look so much like Byrom? And what was wrong with me today? It was like I could watch myself starting to spiral, and then I went and dug my heels in deeper. And even seeing that, I couldn’t stop. *Ours. Mate. Find.* And that probably was the best explanation of them all. My wolf was pushing me, and it was making me second-guess my decisions.

Stop, I seethed. My wolf needed to calm the fuck down.

“How’s that your job?” I asked halfway down the path.

“The tree? It’s not. It’s the nice thing to do.”

"No. You said you would take me because it is your job. Explain."

"You really don't want to have this conversation now. Let's get you settled in." That was so not going to fly.

"No. I don't think so." I stopped in my tracks. "How am I your job?" Because before it was curiosity and now? Now I saw he was trying to evade the entire thing, which meant it was important and probably something I should've known.

"Fine. You are my brother's fated. And don't argue with me about it, because it is fact."

"That doesn't explain anything."

"I'm my brother's Beta. My job is to keep the Alpha family safe, and you wandering around looking for a way into the omega dorm, for whatever your reason, is not safe. And don't even try to argue you're not family, because I'm not going there." He started walking again. "I won't wait for you."

"Fine." I jogged up to him. "It's not like I'm the one being the jerk." I lied. I totally was, but I couldn't bring myself to stop. "Byrom deserves better."

"Bullshit. Fate brings you exactly who you deserve." And that was the last thing he said directly to me, just showing me to my room and mumbling to the person at the door that he'd take care of the paperwork after he finished with Hank's tree.

I crumpled onto the bed, hating what I'd just done and not knowing how or if it was even possible to fix it. My wolf was clawing at me from the inside, clamoring to get out, my bones aching as he tried to force himself through. Screw it. I could go for a run. Maybe it would even help.

I left my boots by the bed and went out back, throwing my clothing on the ground as my wolf took over.

Mate. Find. Claim.

Yeah, that wasn't going to happen. I pushed myself forward, demanding control of our body, four legs and all, and took off in the opposite direction my wolf had wanted to go.

I ran and ran and ran. The more I ran, the more challenging each step was, my wolf trying to force me to turn around, to find our mate.

Our mate.

He was my mate. And that was the worst part. I knew it to be true, but I was afraid of what that meant.

Mate. Ours. Mate.

I pushed to run faster, and then suddenly I couldn't run any more. Shit. I couldn't even walk. My wolf jumped to the forefront and halted, picking our head up and scenting the air.

Bad.

Bad? What did he mean by bad? He flashed a picture of Rance in my mind and brought back the memories of that first day. He hated me. Worse than that, he hated Byrom. Best case scenario, he was out here crossing our paths as a coincidence.

Bad, my wolf repeated. *Evil. Bad. Followed.*

Fuck.

Run, he begged, and I gave him the reins, letting him have control. He sensed the danger before I did. Maybe—just maybe he could get us out of this.

Chapter Twenty-Two

Byrom

I ran so far and so fast that my paws hurt from the effort of it. So many trees and branches slapped across my face, stinging my eyes. My lungs burned.

Thank goodness my territory was vast, and I could run for hours and get away from my problems. I knew it was reckless to travel so far away from my pack without letting my Betas know where I was going. But I couldn't help myself. I needed the space.

I loved Cord. But I didn't know how to help him accept his place as the Alpha Omega. I knew in my heart that it was where he needed to be. I just needed him to know it as well.

When I hit the edge of the territory, I stopped before crossing the line. I didn't need to breach the perimeter and start even more trouble.

I turned around, standing at the edge of my territory. A new Alpha, without its mate, could never rule successfully. I needed an Omega at my side to balance me, to balance the pack. But I would accept no other omega than Cord; knowing he was my fated mate meant my wolf wouldn't accept anyone else.

If he didn't want the position, I couldn't force him. I wouldn't force him.

Time. I needed more time with him. But time was not on my side. The full moon was approaching, and no Alpha had gone so long without a mate in the history of our pack or others, as far as I knew. I'd been so foolish to think I could do this on my own. I was twice the Alpha with Cord by my side.

I longed for the wisdom of my father to help me. But he wasn't there.

I began my trek back to the packhouse. I couldn't be away long, no matter how much I wanted to be. My paws ached along with my heart. It took me some time to get back to the packhouse. I found myself walking in the wrong direction, and I had to correct my course.

My mind was not where it should have been.

When I got back to the packhouse, I didn't bother shifting back. I crawled on to the deck and lay on the wood. I didn't deserve the comfort of my bed right now. I needed the simplicity of my wolf's mind rather than the complicated mess that came with my human form.

Later, I could shift back and face my problems head on. But now, I needed to rest. I needed to give myself over to my wolf.

I closed my eyes, but sleep didn't come easily.

It was hours before I finally rested.

I awoke sometime later, just as tired as I had been when I laid down. Fear clutched at my chest, and panic rose within me.

But why? For what?

There was no threat to me immediately. The backyard was empty, the packhouse quiet. It was the middle of the night, and everyone was asleep.

Still, the panic came in waves. It seemed far off, like it wasn't me that was being threatened. It was more like a signal that I was picking up.

Cord.

My mate was in danger!

I howled out in alarm and took off toward the omega dorm.

Chapter Twenty-Three

Cord

I was being followed. I'd been so worried about my pity party for one that I didn't follow any of the training I'd had, and I was the prey, but not in the sexy way when Byrom and I played this game. No. This time, it was life and death—my life. And Rance had all of the advantages. I wasn't even sure exactly where we were in relation to the rest of the pack.

My wolf was no longer chatting or even conversing with me. He was just running. Every once in a while, he'd catch a scent and head off in a different direction. I didn't understand all that he was doing, and I didn't need to. He was protecting us, whereas I was the one getting us in danger. Lyle had been right during training when he said I needed to be more in tune with my wolf.

In retrospect, his desire to shift and find Byrom probably was more than just missing him. Had I listened, I might not be in this mess, running for my life and getting nowhere fast.

My wolf jumped over a log, landing in a puddle, our paws sinking slightly into the mud. We couldn't afford being slowed down by mud. We needed to get home.

Not the dorms, but my real home, Byrom. I needed to get to Byrom and not even just for him to help me destroy Rance, but to tell him I was sorry, to beg him to take me back, to make things better.

Instead, I was probably going to die in the woods with him thinking I hated him or was ambivalent to him or whatever he translated my irrational behavior to mean.

I sucked as a wolf.

Worse…I sucked as a mate.

Another abrupt halt followed by a change in direction and a small cabin—no, shack came into view, one I'd never seen before. Shit, had we left pack lands? *Traps*, I warned my wolf as the mammoth metal contraption came into sight. The last thing we needed was to get caught in a bear trap and be sitting ducks or dead ducks.

My heart thumped against my chest, my paws raw, my legs no longer able to keep up the speed when none of it mattered anymore. A wolf landed on me, his jaw around my neck. Not Rance. No. This scent was different—muskier.

He meant business.

"Shift!" Rance's voice bellowed out from the shack. "Shift now, you piece of shit." Though Rance was an alpha, and one of Byrom's Betas, his command didn't hold the power necessary to force my wolf to shift.

I refused. Shifting to my human form would only mean

my neck was broken easier. Fuck that.

Rance pulled out a gun.

“I said shift!” A click came from the gun. “Get off him, Danny.”

The wolf loosened his teeth and snarled as he backed away from me.

“Now shift or I’ll shoot your paw—then another—and another—until…you get the picture.” Yeah, I got the picture all right. He was a psychotic freak on top of being a jealous piece of shit.

I forced a shift, not sure what else to do. At least if I could talk, I might be able to buy some time. Disobeying him would only bring torture before my death. Shit, what if he planned to torture me either way? I recalled the way he’d treated me when I was first captured by the pack. Rance wouldn’t hold back.

Byrom. I’m sorry.

“Wh-wh-why?” I asked, not getting off the ground. I did not want to freak him out and get shot by accident. That would put a real damper to my buying-myself-time plan.

“Why do you think? I should be alpha. Byrom, weak-ass Byrom, thinks that you are his mate. You’re nothing but a human in fur. You know nothing of our ways, and he? He disregards our ways at his convenience. I should’ve killed you that first day,” he seethed. I knew he hated Byrom, but the depth of his hatred…I just couldn’t fathom the darkness that lived within him to feel that way about anything or anyone.

“Shift, Danny. Let’s get his sorry ass contained.” The wolf snapped his jaws at me again and shifted into a man not much older than myself, one I didn’t recognize. “Grab his arms behind his back,” he commanded. “And don’t think about shifting. I’ll shoot you where you stand.”

The man obeyed and pretty much pushed me into the shack, where I was bound not only by my hands and feet, but also around my neck, I assumed to keep me from shifting. Fuckers.

“What do you think he’ll fetch for a price?” Rance put the gun in his backpack.

“You only need that when it’s a fair fight.” What was it they said about never poking a bear? Whatever it was was accurate, because he backhanded me so hard the fact that I didn’t lose a tooth was a freaking miracle.

“I don’t know. If we could sell him as a breeder, he’d be worth more.” His spit hit my chest. Ewwww.

“Why can’t we?” Rance asked. “He’s got breeder hips. I bet some alphas would pay top dollar for a piece of that.”

“Scent him, Rance. It’s faint, but it’s there.”

Rance came over and took in a deep breath and spit. “Well, fuck me. You had to go get knocked up, didn’t you, scum?” Slap. This time on the other cheek.

I was pregnant. No. It couldn’t be. I mean, it could. We did the things that make babies happen, but Byrom would’ve scented it if these guys did, right? That was a thing?

“Is there a market for the kid?” Rance kicked my ribcage. I hated the fucker.

“And who will keep him until that happens? You know his alpha is going to be looking.”

No. No. No. Byrom couldn’t come looking. Not with a gun in play. Rance was not going to play fair.

“He needs to be long gone, not chilling for nine months,” the man Rance called Danny continued as if they were talking about a work schedule or what to buy for dinner, not what to do with my baby.

My baby. I was having a baby. At least if I made it out of here alive, I would. Although if they were going to sell me, maybe death was the better of the two options.

“After I take over the pack, it’s not like there will be anyone to come looking.” Rance wanted the pack. Of course, this was about that. What a power-hungry piece of shit.

“Too risky,” Danny countered. “Even if everything works according to plans and we become pack Alphas, we’ll still need time. I say we take him to a dark healer and fix the problem and get a good price for him.”

And that explained why Danny was here. He was looking to take over his pack the way Rance was looking to take over ours. Ours. They were mine. And what did I do? I acted like a teenage brat and led their traitor straight to me.

“They will be our packs, and under our leadership, we’ll be the power players. Between the two of us, we can outmaneuver all the others. I'll find a dark healer."

"No need. I know a guy." He looked me up and down. "We'll get rid of that baby tonight and take him to auction in the morning."

"And then on to phase two."

Dark healer. My body shook as the reality of what they just said set in. They wanted to kill my baby.

I'm so sorry, little one. Daddy's so sorry.

Chapter Twenty-Four

Byrom

I ran as fast as I possibly could through the woods, following the scent I'd found just outside of Cord's bedroom window. There was Cord's scent, and another that I recognized as Rance, and another I couldn't place.

Footsteps followed me, and I recognized my trusted Betas immediately. Lyle, Gio, and Kade. They must have sensed the danger and responded. Other members of our pack followed beside us, Laurence, Taylor, Mia, and Lissy.

They all responded instinctively to the danger that threatened the pack's Alpha Omega.

It didn't take us long to reach a shack where Rance and Cord's scent was the strongest. A light glowed from underneath the makeshift door, the makeshift door of new wood. This was what Rance had been doing with the supplies. He basically threw his plan in my face, and I pushed it to the side.

I could've prevented this, and instead, I allowed my omega, my mate, to fall right into danger.

Lyle stepped in front of me, indicating for me to stop, but my wolf wouldn't listen. Cord was in there, and he needed me. It was my fault there was a shack for him to be in and my responsibility to get him out safely. He might not have chosen me, but I was his until his dying breath, and I'd be damned if that wasn't sixty years in the future.

This wasn't an unknown intruder that I could let my Betas deal with without me. My mate was in there, and I wasn't going to stand by some place safe to watch. Not that I'd allow that on a normal day no matter the protocol. I pushed past Lyle, just as Gio ran past me.

For a moment, I thought Gio was going to try to stop me, try being the operative word. To my surprise, he jumped. His four paws hit the rickety door like a battering ram, busting through the plywood.

Inside, Cord sat on a chair. He had his hands tied in front of him, his neck bound. Rance stood over him, an expression of pure hatred on his face, almost daring me to try something. Did he not know how this was going to end? There were zero scenarios where he would make it out of this alive.

I didn't give him a chance to say anything. As soon as I was within range, I leapt. My teeth sank into whatever flesh I could get a hold of. I bit down and tore at his arm. I pulled him away from Cord. He needed to be as far away from my mate as possible. My wolf wanted him dead, and I did, too, but first we needed to get him safely away from my mate.

Rance tried to push me off, but I wasn't letting up. He

was weaker than me on a normal day, but with Cord's life at stake…his attempts were beyond futile. Out of the corner of my eye, I saw Lyle and Gio surrounding Cord, keeping him safe from the other wolf that was with Rance. I didn't recognize him, and I didn't have a chance to think about who he was.

Kade squared off with him in a fight, and I trusted my Betas to keep Cord from danger, Mia and Lissy circling them. He wasn't getting anywhere. There was no one fiercer than my cousin and our schoolteacher.

Rance shifted, and I lost my grip on him. His wounds didn't heal with the shift, though, which gave me the advantage. I saw my chance, and I took it, sinking my teeth into the scruff of his neck and pinning him to the ground.

He fought back, but I was the strong wolf. I always had been, which was why he'd never challenged me and instead went after my omega. Coward.

I held him against the ground until he submitted. He whimpered from the pain, and the taste of blood filled my mouth, but still I held him. I couldn't trust his submission, not after what he'd pulled.

My pack alphas answered the call to protect their Alpha Omega and circled around me, each shifted in their wolf form. There would be no trial for Rance, no chance for him to explain. His actions were enough. Rance had committed the ultimate crime. He kidnapped a mate of a pack member, the Alpha no less, in order to do him harm. I was going to end his existence.

Cord was at my side, his hand on my back, letting me know he was safe. *End him.* His voice rang through my head. He might think he was too human for our pack, but his words were all wolf.

Rance's end came swiftly. My jaws clamped down on his neck until he took his last breath. I tossed him to the side. I'd spend no more time on that traitor. Let the crows have him.

I sat back, and the other wolf that worked with Rance began to scramble away, out of Kade's hold, everyone's focus on Rance's death. He tried to take off, but another set of wolves showed up. I recognized the Northbay Pack scent, but I had never met their alpha.

I growled, putting myself between the other wolves and Cord, my pack falling in behind me, each of them keeping their future Alpha Omega safe.

Talk to them, Cord. Strength radiated from Cord in a way I'd never seen, and it made me proud.

I shifted back to my human form, and the other pack Alpha did the same, my pack still protecting Cord in their fur but no longer baring their teeth.

No one said a word.

Rance lay on the ground to the side of us, his wounds bleeding into the dirt.

The other traitor's eyes shifted between the Northbay Alpha and me. Did he think he was getting out of this? I'd be happy to watch him bleed out as well, but his wounds weren't deep enough; soon, I'd remedy that—

with or without his Alpha's permission.

"Do you know this wolf?" the Alpha asked, gesturing to Rance.

I rolled my shoulders back and lifted my chin. My pack stood behind me, ready to do whatever I asked of them. "Rance was one of my Betas, but he has betrayed me and our pack. He has been punished for his crimes."

The other Alpha gestured to the beta that worked with Rance. "He's one my pack members and also a betrayer."

"How can I believe you?" I said. "How do I know you haven't orchestrated this?"

Cord put a hand on my arm and stepped next to me. "Rance told me his plan to pit the two packs against each other so that he and the other beta could take over." Cord placed a shaking hand to his stomach. "He and the other guy were going to have me sold as—as a breeder after they found a Dark Healer."

I growled low in my throat. I was ready to kill Rance again and again for the trouble he'd put my mate through and be done with him, and the other wolf, too. They were snakes, the both of them.

My eyes shifted to Cord's hands briefly. They sat on his belly. *Dark Healer.* Could it be? Was he carrying my pup?

Gio grabbed onto the scruff of the other wolf's neck and wrangled a collar around him. The collar was threaded in silver and forged with the blood of the Alpha, which prevented him from shifting. It was a tactic rarely used on a wolf, only in extreme circumstances. These were extreme.

It was the ultimate insult for a shifter to be collared and leashed in this way.

"Death is too easy on them, but it is what they deserve," the Northbay Alpha said. "To kidnap an omega, the future Alpha Omega, in his condition, I can hardly believe it." He gestured to his Betas at his side. They moved quickly, taking their collared beta that had worked with Rance to try to take us down.

The Alpha stuck out his hand for me to shake. "I'm Dylan. It's a pleasure to meet you. Even if it is under these circumstances."

I eyed him carefully, sniffing the air to find truth radiating from him. No betrayal. No malice.

"I'm Byrom," I said. "This is my Alpha Omega, Cord." No future to it. He was mine.

Cord waved awkwardly. He stuck to my side like glue. If it were up to me, he'd never leave it again.

"I was sorry to hear about your father," Dylan said. "He was a good Alpha."

"Thank you."

"I think it's past time for the two of us to sit down and discuss a few things. We only want to have peace between us. There's a lot we can learn from each other. I know it isn't the ways of the Packs to work with one another, but I think it's time for new Alphas to force a new way."

"I agree," I said. "We would love to meet with you. But that will have to wait for another night. I need to get my omega home and safe."

"Agreed," he said. "I'll send a messenger over in a week's time to coordinate a meeting."

"That's perfect. Thank you," I said.

"You're lucky to have your mate so early in your time as Alpha."

I cocked my head to the side in question. Dylan had been Alpha for longer than I had, though he was the same age as me. "You are unmated?" I said. Though, now that I pieced through his scent, I could sense that he was not.

He nodded. "I have not yet found mine. But it's evident that he is yours, though I don't see any evidence of the mating mark."

"Yes, he is mine."

Cord leaned into me. "I am."

Chapter Twenty-Five

Cord

"I'm so sorry," I said for the four thousandth time, meaning each and every one of them. Byrom didn't respond, just carrying me back to our house, not even stopping at the omega dorms to get my belongings. I didn't need them. I had him, and that was more than enough.

He thought he was taking me home.

I was already there.

We reached the house, and he marched me straight inside and to the bathroom, where he set me down long enough to turn on the shower.

"You smell like him." He growled, and I finally understood. Rance was still with us, and until he was gone gone, we wouldn't be able to move past this.

The human side of me felt guilty for being relieved he was dead. My wolf held no such remorse. He relished the blood.

Once we'd returned from the woods, I'd hoped to go

straight to a bed, but instead we'd found the entire rest of the pack waiting outside when we'd arrived.

They'd all wanted to make sure I was okay. I couldn't believe how relieved I was to see them all, how my wolf howled and danced with delight at being back with our pack after not being sure if we were ever going to see them again. And then Byrom barked out for them to go home, and here we were.

I stepped inside the shower, the water still not yet hot, and started to scrub away, Byrom joining me. We silently lathered up, washing the dirt, the blood, the scent down the drain, and then beginning again just in case we missed something.

"He's gone." I grabbed his hand and took the soap out of it. "He's gone."

"You were almost gone." He pulled me into his arms, holding me tight. "He almost took you from me."

"But he didn't. You stopped him." I kissed his shoulder. "You saved me…you saved us." I placed his hand on my belly. "I didn't know. You have to believe I didn't know."

"I didn't, either. You scented off, but not…it's new." He reached around me and turned off the water. "Stay with me."

"Always. I don't know what was happening…it was like I… I won't leave again. I promise." A shiver ran through me, the chill of standing there dripping wet finally sinking in. "Let me dry you off, alpha mine." His breath hitched as I spoke the words, telling him everything with but three syllables.

Alpha Mine.

And he was and had been. I'd even seen it, felt it, believed it in my core. I'd just been too scared to accept the gift fate had been offering. That time had ended.

I pushed open the shower and grabbed a towel and toweled him off, taking extra care to be gentle knowing that his body had been through a lot.

"Let me." He took the towel from me as I started to dry myself. "Let me take care of you, omega mine."

"Make it real." I spoke softly. "Make me yours for real."

He dropped the towel and cupped my cheeks with both hands. "It has been real since the moment I saw you in the clearing that first day. It was wrong of me to push you into being the pack Alpha Omega."

"I want to be more. I want to wear your mark. I want to take my place by your side both in our lives and in your position in the pack. I'll make mistakes…so many mistakes, but I will always give my all."

"You don't have to," he reiterated.

"Do you want me as your mate…for real? Do you want me to wear your mark? Do you want to wear mine?"

"More than my next breath."

"Then please, alpha, make it so. I love you, and

imagining living even one second on this earth without you tears me apart inside."

He dropped his hands from my cheeks and scooped me up. "I love you, Cord." He kissed me far too briefly for my liking and brought me into his—no, our bedroom and gently settled me on the bed, his body quickly covering mine. "There is nothing I want more than to make you mine."

His lips crashed into mine all raw and passionate, and I met him with equal force. I needed to taste him, to feel him, to scent like him. I needed it all. My arms held him close, not wanting even a centimeter between us.

My gums were already hurting, our bodies not yet joined, my wolf clamoring to sink his teeth into Byrom, to mark him as ours.

Mate. Mark. Mine.

"Byrom," I whimpered against his lips, and he separated enough for me to speak. I hated the distance. "My wolf—can't wait—need you inside me now."

"Let me get—"

"No, I'm already ready, my gums hurt, my wolf…" He met my eyes, his own just as feral as mine felt. "Please."

"Omega mine," he kissed me and pushed himself up, "roll over."

"I want to mark you at the same time." It was so human for me to want to face him. I knew this, and I didn't care.

"Hips up." He reached behind me and grabbed a pillow, sliding it under my hips and not even questioning my desire to be so human in such a wolf time. "Are you sure you're ready…? I can—"

"Now," I pleaded.

He lined himself up and pushed inside of me far too slowly for my liking. I was ready…so very ready, and I bucked my hips, finishing the job. "That's better," I sassed, pulling him down to me, needing to kiss him.

"Much," he agreed and kissed me as he slid in and out of me, our bodies in sync, our arousals growing, our wolves so close I could hear his echoing my own. Or was it mine echoing his? It didn't matter. They were saying the same thing, *mate*, and it was the most glorious sound.

It didn't take long before the aching became more and my canines broke through, nipping his lips a little too roughly, the tinge of blood on my tongue emboldening my wolf to take over, yanking my head from his and sinking his teeth into Byrom's neck as I exploded, my cum shooting between us as a sharp pain on my shoulder turned to immense pleasure. He was marking me. He was mine.

His knot filled me, only heightening the pleasure.

"Mine." I kissed where I'd just marked.

"Mine." He did the same and collapsed on top of me, the feeling of his weight on me only intensifying the joy that was flowing through me.

"Will they care that you're marked in the wrong spot?" I

asked after we caught our breaths, suddenly seeing the possible ramifications of what I'd asked him to do.

"I don't care. You're what is important to me. I'd already told Lyle the pack would be his if you chose a human life."

"You did? When?"

"When I first knew you were mine." He kissed my cheek and rolled us over so I was now on top. "It has always been you. I refused to mate waiting for you. I didn't know it at the time, but in hindsight, I always knew you were out there for me."

How had I not known this? I'd been so worried about fitting a stupid mold, and all he cared about was me being in his life. I didn't deserve this man.

"You don't have to wait anymore." I licked his mark, my wolf stupid proud of the thing. Who was I kidding? I was, too. He was mine.

"I love you, omega mine."

"As I love you." With all that I was.

Chapter Twenty-Six

Byrom

It had been a long while since our pack had this much to celebrate. Just a handful of full moons ago, we'd abruptly lost our beloved pack Alpha and many of the pack leaders, including the Alpha Omega. The loss had left us unbalanced and weak. Then Rance and his friend wreaked havoc on the pack, destroying morale and causing disruption.

But now, today, just a week after Rance's death, and a week since my heart nearly stopped when I found out Cord had been kidnapped, I was here in the sunlight of an open clearing with my mate.

The trees rustled around us as a light breeze swept through the area. We were surrounded by our pack, our friends and our family. Lyle stood at my side. Lissy stood beside Cord.

We'd asked Mia to officiate the ceremony, since she had become friends with Cord.

The parents hurried to get their pups to settle down so that we could begin.

It was tradition not to see the mate before the ceremony. Cord and I were both blindfolded when we were led to the clearing. I knew he was close, though. I could scent him, his cherry blossom scent now sweeter with each passing day of his pregnancy. His belly was still flat, but that didn't stop me from caressing it constantly.

"Hold out your hands," Mia said.

I did. My fingers bumping into Cord's. He was directly across from me now. I could sense him that close to me. He still smelled of new growth, like the forest after a rain, but also a hint of new life, the life of our child that he carried.

"Clasp your hands together," Mia said, and we did. "A wolf is led by our senses. Hearing and smell. It is easy for others to believe what they see and nothing else. But the wolf knows you must trust in what you feel. Both of you can sense your mate beside you."

I squeezed Cord's hand. His heartbeat kicked up a notch, and my own raced to catch up.

"You have bound yourselves together with your mating mark, and with these words, you will bind yourselves together for life for all your pack to see. Alpha, do you accept this omega as yours and yours alone to lead with you as your Alpha Omega?"

"I do," I said.

Mia turned to Cord. "Cord, do you accept this alpha, as your mate and pack Alpha, to lead at his side as his Alpha Omega?"

“I do.”

“And now the two of you will see each other for the first time as mates, and Alpha and Alpha Omega of the Greycoast Pack. You are now one for the pack.”

The blindfolds were taken off.

I saw Cord with new eyes. The future for us and the pack looking brighter than it had in a long time.

I kissed him, and the pack around us cheered. This was our future.

“I proudly introduce you to our Alpha Omega,” Mia announced, all official, just a second before hugging Cord. “Love you, Alpha Omega. Thank you for choosing our pack,” she whispered in my mate’s ear and then kissed both of our cheeks.

I took my mate’s hand, and we stepped to the front of the platform as each of my Betas stepped forward and bared their necks to us, followed by the other single shifters and family groups. Unlike the night the pack welcomed Cord into our fold, this wasn’t an acceptance; this was a congratulations, and the tears in so many of the pack member’s eyes had my mate’s own eyes releasing his tears—happy tears.

After the last wolf shared our joy in the traditional way, I whistled to catch everyone’s attention.

“Greycoast Pack, upon mating, it is traditional for us to run together, to celebrate with our wolves, but today we add a new tradition, a tradition that doesn’t exclude our young who cannot yet run, a tradition that Cord brings from the human realm and one, I believe, you will all enjoy."

"He makes it sound so scandalous," Cord teased as the Betas, Lissy, and Mia came into the clearing carrying tables filled with enough food for the county. "We are going to eat, and if we are so inclined, we might even dance."

And that was just what we did. We ate and danced and laughed, the entire pack as one big family, and just as the young were getting sleepy and nothing but the crumbs were left of the cake, I whistled again.

"Brother and Sister wolves, we have joined as one of the flesh with our marks, vowed our commitment before our pack, and celebrated as humans. Now we run, led by our Alpha Omega."

Cord jumped off the platform shifting mid-air, not caring about his clothing, having somehow removed his boots unnoticed while I spoke. He'd been working on that shift tirelessly, and watching him do it with confidence in front of our entire pack had me puffing out my chest with pride.

I joined him, running after him, glad to see he waited for the pack at the edge of the clearing, my fast little wolf.

Mate. I brushed our noses together as I reached him.

Alpha Mine. He licked my snout. *Run with me.*

Always.

We ran as a pair, leading our pack around the perimeter

of our land, Dylan and his pack standing on the hill just over the line, howling their congratulations, another new thing my omega inadvertently brought to our pack. We were no longer an isolated group; we had a pack that formed a brothership with ours in a way our kind had never seen. It was new, and we were still figuring out our way, but it was a solid beginning, and both our packs' futures looked brighter because of it.

Cord called over to them, and I joined him, shortly followed by the entire pack. And then something amazing happened, something that would've made my fathers so proud. For the first time in the history of our pack, another pack joined us in celebration, running side by side with our wolves along our borders, wolves crossing the lines as if they didn't exist—all because of Cord.

He might've worried he wasn't enough for the pack—he was too human or too new to our way of life or what have you—but in this single act, he showed two packs that fate had sent our pack their perfect Alpha Omega.

And by some miracle I got to call him *Mine.*

Epilogue

Cord

"The books are done." I looked up from my desk in the office I now shared with Byrom. It was hardly the traditional way of doing things as an Alpha, but whatever. It worked for us, and the pack was thriving.

"What would I ever do without you, omega mine?"

"Your own accounting," I teased, pushing myself up from my chair, the chair I barely fit in, and waddled around my desk. Yes. I had officially reached the waddling portion of my pregnancy along with the *I'm so done and am pretty positive I'm going to give birth to a fifty-pound baby* portion as well.

Fair to say I was ready to meet our child.

Byrom whistled at me, his sweet way of pretending I was still hot. I. Was. Not. Between the dark circles forming under my eyes and my cankles—oh, my stupid cankles—zero people would consider me anything above a five, and the five would be generous.

"Am I interrupting something?" Lyle stood in the

doorway. Damn, his circles were as bad as mine.

“Your twin thought a whistle would make me feel less unappealing.” I stuck my tongue out at Byrom playfully.

“My brother’s no fool. He knows hotness when he sees it,” Lyle teased back, the humor never reaching his eyes. He’d been like that for the past couple of days, and I couldn’t blame him. Not with all the crap being thrown at him, knowing he was going to be acting as pack Alpha for at least two weeks after the baby was born. Sure, Byrom would still be there if he needed it, but pack tradition had two-week babymoons, for lack of a better term, the norm. I was not sad about that. As much as they said parents knew what to do instinctually, I didn’t fully believe it.

I’d never known my real parents, and the foster parents were far from role models. If instinct didn’t kick in, I had nothing to fall back on, either.

Byrom and Lyle tried to discover who my parents were, with no real success. The only evidence they could find was an article about bear traps being illegally set and two wolves, a dog, and a deer being killed by them. Chances were the wolves were my parents, killed by the same kind of traps that almost got me that night all those months ago.

“Your flattery will get you everywhere.” I winked at Lyle, wishing I could do something to alleviate his stress.

The baby began their daily gymnastics time, and I waddled over to Byrom as fast as I could. His favorite thing was to feel our child move, and if I could help him experience that joy by racing over there, as ridiculous as I looked, I was all in.

"Gymnastics time?" He practically jumped over his desk to meet me part way as Lyle began to crack up.

"Just wait until it's your omega." And just like that, his laughter died.

"Brother, he meant nothing by it." Byrom's hands were on my belly, feeling our little guy move, but his entire focus was on his brother. Shit. What had I inadvertently done?

"I'm sorry, Lyle. I didn't mean anything by it. I was trying to be silly." I couldn't see him from the angle I was at, and I rotated around to see his face showing nothing—no sadness, no anger, no joy—nothing.

"It's not your fault, Alpha Omega. I just have some pack things I'm dealing with."

"If Byrom needs to work when the baby comes, I'm not *that* omega. Promise." Shit, if it would make it better for Lyle, I'd take on some of the tasks. I'd be like those baby-wearing super omegas they had in the baby gear advertisements.

"You, my dear sweet brother." It still warmed my heart every time he called me that. It probably always would. Going from no family to a huge family, for that was what my pack was, had been one of the best things that ever happened to me. Mating Byrom and growing our child were the only things that topped it. "You have nothing to apologize for, nor nothing to make up for."

"Lyle is working with another pack on some antiquated laws. It's something only he can do, and he'll be amazing at it. He can be so ornery even I don't want to be around him, and I love the guy."

I went to ask him what that even meant as my pants stuck to me. No, not stuck, really, just wet.

Fuck.

"Honey…we should call Lissy, I think."

"Is something wrong?" Byrom asked as Lyle whipped out his phone, already seeing what Byrom was so oblivious to.

"I'm just having our baby." But where were the contractions? "Or at least I think my water just broke. Maybe I just peed myself. That wouldn't be embarrassing, not at all."

"I told you it was fine. You didn't need to pee to get me distracted," Lyle teased and then went back to his phone call.

"I want to change before we go," I whined, and Byrom scooped me up as if I weren't the size of a house. "Now you'll have to change, too."

"We're only going to the bedroom, love. Lissy will meet us there."

"I'll let her in and be on my way," Lyle called from behind us. "Call me when the mess is cleaned up." He chuckled.

"Aren't you cleaning it up, brother?" I bantered back, loving the rich laughter pouring over him. At least I put a smile on his face.

Byrom carried me to the bedroom and helped me out of my wet clothing. I didn't bother putting on new. Why bother if our baby was coming? How different I was about the whole clothing thing from the first time I met Byrom. I'd been so embarrassed, and now? Now I wore them as little as possible.

"Shouldn't I be having contractions?" I asked as we waited for Lissy. "Like, don't they usually come first?" A knock at our door startled me. "Please let that be her."

And it was. Thank gods.

"A little birdie told me it's baby time." She came in with a small old-fashioned medical bag, the kind you'd see on westerns, and looking just as worn as if it were from back in the day.

"My water broke, but I've had no contractions."

"It's perfectly normal. They'll start coming soon enough. Your wolf is just protecting you as long as he can." I wanted to ask her what she meant by that. A contraction chose that time to come barreling into me instead, and I nearly collapsed by the sudden pain of it all. "Looks like your baby will be here any time now."

How was she so fucking cheerful?

I caught my breath and, with Byrom's help, made it to our bed. I didn't want to be caught off guard like that again. I so very much did not need to be falling on top of everything else.

"What about the whole contractions start out weak thing?" I huffed as I climbed into bed.

"They did. Your wolf just took the pain for you." Whoa. How had I not known that was possible? "It's at the point he no longer—"

Another contraction hit, but I at least half-expected it.

"The baby was kicking." I still didn't understand any of this other than labor hurt, which I'd known, but not to what extent.

"How about we get you ready to push next time and I can teach you the birds and the bees later?" She turned her attention to Byrom, who was brushing the hair off my brow. "I apologize, Alpha. Our Alpha Omega is such a natural, I forgot that this would be foreign to him."

"I will forgive you if you get this baby out of me." I wasn't kidding. The contractions were building again, and this time the need to push with it. "You said I can push," I reminded her as I focused all of the pain and energy into pushing.

This continued for a solid ten minutes when it changed, my body starting to burn, Byrom and Lissy encouraging me, telling me how amazing I was doing, that our child was almost here. The burning grew, the agony multiplied, and then the most glorious sound rang through my ears…our baby's cry.

"You did so well, love." Byrom kissed my forehead, his voice thick with emotion. "Our baby…he's beautiful."

Lissy placed him on my chest. "Here is your son, our heir apparent. He is perfect."

I looked down at his little face, still not cleaned up yet, and every worry I had about whether I could be a good enough father vanished. I loved this little being so much there was no way I could be anything but the best father for him. He needed me, and I was not going to let him down.

"Thank you." Byrom slid onto the bed beside me. "Thank you for making me the happiest man in the world."

"Impossible, alpha mine. I'm the happiest man in the world."

The End

Mpreg Titles by Jena Wade

Greycoast Pack with Lorelei M. Hart

Finding His Purpose

Finding His Pack

Finding His Potential

Finding His Passion

Lights Of Fate

Blue

Purple

Bake Sale Bachelors

Sugar Cookie Kiss (Jena Wade)

SnickerDoodle Sweetie (Lorelei M. Hart)

Gingerbread Greetings (Leyla Hunt)

Apple Pie Pair (Jena Wade)

Meat Pie Match
(Lorelei M. Hart)

Cherry Pie Charm (Leyla Hunt)

Lemon Meringue Love (Summer Chase)

Tall Tails

Unexpected Packages

Rochdale Security

The Bodyguard's Charge
The Bodyguard's Relationship
The Bodyguard's Professor (with Lorelei M. Hart)
The Bodyguard's Assistant
The Bodyguard's Technician
The Bodyguard's Christmas Surprise

Millerstown Moments

Dashboard Lights
Crying Out Loud (with Lorelei M. Hart)
Anything For Love
Life is a Lemon (with Lorelei M. Hart)
Box Set with Heaven Can Wait short story

Vale Valley

Picture Purrfect
The Cat & The Hound

Dragons Series

Dragon's Fire
Dragon's Ice
Dragon's Stone
Dragon's Jewel
Dragon's Spark

Directions Series

Up to Code
Down to Earth
Back to You

Shorts
Alpha Student
Alpha Doctor

Jena Wade

Jena lives in Michigan with her husband, two dogs, and three children. By day she works as a web developer and at night she writes. She was born and raised on a farm and spends most of her free time outdoors, playing in the garden or tending to her landscaping.

Find out more about the author at http://www.thejenawade.com/.

Follow Jena on Facebook (https://www.facebook.com/jena.wade.7528) or Twitter (https://twitter.com/thejenawade).

Subscribe to Jena's Newsletter (https://mailchi.mp/9b658a089de7/signup)(she promises not to spam).

Printed in Great Britain
by Amazon

82291002R00116